Sleeping on the Terrace

by Guy Winters

DEDICATION

This book would not be possible without the generosity of Joscelyn Hayes and David Schultz. I simply could not have completed this work without their attention to detail and dedicated support.

A special note to the reader:
This story is intended for a mature audience only. It contains adult situations and graphic language and is not intended, nor allowed to be read by individuals under the age of 18.

.

Here's what others have said about this book:

"What a wonderful, caring story, so beautifully told."

"An understanding and caring romance that takes the reader on a journey of trust, trust that lets a relationship grow and become something more than just the sum of the story's "parts"."

"Love this story...the pace...the sensuality...the difference...the passion!"

"I love how your characters grow with each new chapter, and how you have their relationships grow with them. They are such a wonderful group of interesting and together people. I do so enjoy the way your dialogue brings the reader into the story. The characters are all so upbeat and the sort of people I would love to be involved with. Their caring, understanding, and acceptance is admirable."

[This} Would Make A Great SitCom...in a 'normal' world. The characters make the story jump, and the action made it feel like I was there. You make caring about all of these characters easy and understanding their motivations easier. Love the movie, play, and book references, especially *the Princess Bride*. Incredible writing, as usual."

This book was first published in chapter format under the title of *Sleeping on the Terrace* with an electronic copyright of 2013.

An electronic version of this book, published by Buckhorn Press is available at
www.Smashwords.com

=ONE=

It was sunny out and Jason had just finished stacking all the boxes the movers dumped in the middle of his new apartment. He was bushed. How can it be this hot and not melt glass? He wiped his brow and realized that August can be brutal in Virginia.

He looked at the thermometer on the wall outside the terrace door. It was already well beyond ninety and the day was far from over. He picked up the phone and dialed the building manager.

"Hello, any word yet on when the AC guy is going to show up and fix my unit?"

He nodded as if the person on the other end of the conversation could see it.

"Okay, right, can you call them again and nudge them my way? Thanks."

At least the terrace isn't on the sunny side of the building.

"I need something to drink," he muttered as he walked towards the refrigerator in his small kitchen.

With a cool glass of iced tea in hand Jason

headed for the terrace to rest. He looked through the screen door that led to his side of the terrace. It wasn't much to write home about. It wasn't very deep, perhaps eight feet or so, and it ran the full length of the building.

But it was covered. That was a plus. The cover provided a modest amount of protection from the sun and rain. There was a short wall that bisected the area in half so that the two apartments on this side of the third floor shared equal parts of the terrace. Fences make good neighbors, he mused.

He was hoping to catch a breeze while waiting for the repairman. He sat down on a ragged looking wicker chaise lounge and within minutes, in spite of the heat, he began to doze off.

Moments later he heard the neighbor's terrace screen door slide open. He decided to keep his eyes shut and play 'possum'. Maybe if he pretended to be asleep they wouldn't notice him.

Standing next to the low wall that separated the two areas on the common terrace, his neighbor waited while Jason appeared to be sleeping on the chaise. Then, as if caught by a sudden idea, his neighbor quickly dashed back inside their apartment.

Jason relaxed again with a sigh and settled further into the cushions. Apparently playing 'possum' worked.

Unfortunately, his reward for 'faking it' was short lived because he heard his neighbor's screen door slide open again. A moment or two later the neighbor returned and, to his surprise, they stepped over the low fence that divided the terrace and walked up to him lying on the chaise.

Jason barely opened his eyes and peeked through

narrow slits. What he saw surprised him. Standing at the foot of his lounger was a very pretty woman holding a bottle of red nail polish. Well, in for a penny, in for a pound. Besides, why spoil her fun.

She sat down cross-legged at his feet, opened the bottle of nail polish, and began to paint his toenails. He watched her carefully. She glanced up several times to make sure he was still asleep. When he didn't flinch she seemed satisfied that she hadn't disturbed him and she resumed her prank.

Jason slowly opened his eyes again and watched his neighbor grin as she painted his toenails red. Hmm, very pretty. He admired what he could see through his nearly closed eyes. He tried to keep as still as possible even when she inadvertently tickled him.

Once done, she picked up a pair of white sandals with four-inch heels and slowly slipped the shoes on his feet.

A few minutes later, Jason opened his eyes and glanced down to see his neighbor sitting cross-legged near his feet and grinning like a Cheshire cat.

He looked down at his feet and then to her. He grinned awkwardly and admired her work.

"Nice color." He raised his foot up to inspect his toes. "Nice shoes, too. I'm surprised that you had a pair that fit." He sat his feet on the terrace floor and starting to stand up. He walked casually to the terrace door that led into his apartment. He turned to see her still sitting on the floor with a look of shock on her face.

"What? I bet you expected me to stumble or fall didn't you?" His mouth curled into an impish grin then he turned and walked inside.

Totally surprised, she got up and followed him to the doorway. "Hey!"

"Want something cool to drink? I think the afternoon sun is still warming up the place. Or perhaps it's just the nail polish?"

She folded her arms across her chest. "You've worn heels before, haven't you?"

"Once or twice, but never in front of anyone else. You're the first. You can have water, iced tea, or a soda? You pick."

"Iced tea please." She leaned against the doorframe. "You move well in them. They look very cute on you."

"Thank you." Jason filled up two glasses and walked back to sit by the couch in front of the television. "Join me." He gestured for her to sit as he sat on a chair nearby.

She took the glass he offered and sat tentatively, sipping her tea. Jason glanced at her and he could see that curiosity was getting the best of her.

"Are you into cross-dressing?"

"You see that's what bugs me about the whole social construct. Women can wear pants and shirts and ties and it's not cross-dressing, it's considered cute or sexy. Men can't wear dresses or panties or high heels because it's considered feminine and perverted. Therefore it's negatively referred to as cross-dressing, transvestitism, or what have you."

"Nice rant but you didn't answer my question."

"I know. I can't find an answer that suits me." He set his feet on the coffee table and crossed his ankles. Then he admired the sandals on his feet. "These shoes do look nice don't they?"

She shook her head and chuckled. "You are

unique."

"Not really. Just open-minded and unwilling to adhere to an antiquated concept of how men and women should or can behave." He paused a moment and looked at her with a big smile. She had incredibly blue eyes.

"Hi, I'm Jason." He stood up and offered his hand. "I just moved in this morning. Apparently we share a terrace, well sort of share."

"I'm Rachel, I'm glad to meet you," she replied.

In those four-inch heels he stood several inches above her slender five-foot ten-inch frame. She stood there barefoot and grinned back at him as he sat back down and began to channel surf on the television across the room.

Rachel's mouth twisted into an impish smirk as she sat down cross-legged on the couch and studied him over the rim of her glass of iced tea. He was busy flipping through channels on the television while the sound was muted. He actually wasn't that much taller than she was, and his sandy brown hair had a bit of a curl and an unkempt look about it which she admired. He had a nice face, a warm and inviting smile, and his eyes seemed to twinkle with mischief.

His handshake was firm and warm. She liked that. It was a good sign. The fact that he could not only enjoy her prank but walk comfortably in four-inch heels didn't go unnoticed either. She smiled wistfully. Perhaps her luck was improving...finally.

She traced the rim of her ice tea glass with her finger and looked up at him coyly. "What do you do when you're not walking around in my sandals or sleeping on the terrace?"

Jason turned away from the television and

glanced back at Rachel. "I'd like to say that I'm a writer but that hasn't worked out so well lately. In reality I'm starting work next week teaching English at the community college."

"What do you write about?"

"Mostly commercial stuff...nothing ground breaking."

"Have I read any of your stories?" She knew her collection wasn't extensive but it was growing.

"Probably not, unless you go for romance or erotica."

"Hmmm, I do actually, at least the romance stuff. Do you have a pen name or should I just search under the name Jason?"

"I do, but I'm not ready to share that just yet."

She glanced over to him with a devilish grin. "Feeling a little vulnerable are we?"

"A little. A writer reveals a lot about who they are by what they write and the way they write it. Perhaps I'll share some of my work with you sometime."

"I'd like that."

"And what do you do when you're not painting the toenails of unsuspecting neighbors?"

"I. T."

"You do 'it'? "Seems like an odd job, 'it'."

"Ha, ha, very funny. I.T. Information Technology, I work for a law group downtown keeping the nimrods from crashing their database among other things."

"So I can come to you when my computer goes on the fritz?"

"For a price," she replied, her eyes sparkling. "Like dinner."

"That's an excellent idea. How about I bank some credits and we have dinner out this Saturday? I'd ask you earlier but I still have to sort out all this stuff." He waved towards the stack of boxes on the far wall.

"Need an extra pair of hands? I'd be happy to help."

"No, but thanks for the offer. I didn't do a very good job of labeling so it's really only a puzzle I can decipher."

She smiled and nodded.

Jason put his feet on the floor and unbuckled her sandals. He stood up and then handed them to her with a broad grin. "Thanks."

"Well then," she replied with a winsome smile while draping her sandals over her shoulder, "I'll guess I'll see you Saturday night." She walked out the terrace door with her drink in hand fully intending to use it as an excuse to see him again later if the opportunity presented itself. She felt like her fortunes were suddenly beginning to brighten.

He stood there watching her disappear around the corner. "Great!" Then he glanced down at his naked red toes and smiled.

The following morning came too early for Jason as he walked out of his apartment. He yawned and stretched as he turned to lock his door. He had a nine o'clock meeting and he was already running late.

At the same moment he noticed his neighbor, whom he thought he met the day before as a beautiful woman, step out of the apartment next door. Only now his neighbor was dressed in pants, a shirt and tie, a ball cap, and a nice suit jacket.

He looked very much like a young man casually heading off to work. It could have been her brother were it not for the eyes. They had the same blue intensity that he remembered finding himself lost in yesterday afternoon. Plus the touch of mascara around the corners helped convince him that he was looking at the same person.

Jason nodded in his neighbor's direction and smiled. "Good morning."

"Good morning," she replied, slightly blushing. Her eyes darted around the hallway and looked a little panicky.

"Could you tell Rachel that I'd like to pick her up around six on Saturday. Do you think that will be okay with her?"

He seemed to relax a moment and then he nodded and smiled. "I'm sure it will be fine."

"Great. Thanks."

That afternoon he returned from his last class and opened his front door to find Rachel standing in the terrace doorway holding two cartons of Chinese carryout and sporting a coquettish smile. "Hi. Dinner's ready."

Jason shook his head with a grin and gestured her towards his kitchen.

He opened up one of the cartons. "Umm, Kung-Pao Chicken, my favorite!"

She chuckled. "My lucky guess paid off."

They pulled out plates and flatware and Jason got two beers out of his refrigerator.

He led the way to the terrace door. "Let's take this to the terrace."

A few minutes later, with clean plates piled on a table between the chairs, Jason leaned back in his chair and slowly finished his beer.

"So," she said as nonchalantly as possible, "where were you before you moved here?"

"Cleveland."

"Cleveland? I've never met anyone from Cleveland before," she replied rather energetically.

"Well, I'm not really from Cleveland, that's just where I was last. I come from a military family so we moved around a lot. I guess you could say I'm from the Earth. I suppose that would be more accurate. My dad and mom were both career military and that meant we spent most of our lives living out of a suitcase."

"So how come you didn't follow in their footsteps?"

"They would have liked that a lot but the military life was not for me. I told them so one day when they were pressuring me to enlist and my dad went all 'The Great Santini' on my ass. I walked out on them and lived with my grandmother for a couple of months before college started."

"I stayed in school longer than I expected and fell in love with writing," he continued after a pull on his beer. "I knocked around a bit, tried to sell my stories and eventually I ended up teaching high school English in Cleveland."

"Why did you leave?"

"Bored, and tired of stupid public school administrators who have their heads shoved so far up politician's asses that they haven't seen daylight in years. School systems that cater to the lowest common denominator, students who…."

"Okay, okay, I get it," she said interrupting. "But you're still teaching in public school, albeit it's college instead of high school."

"True," he replied. "I heard someone call it 'thirteenth grade' the other day and the description wasn't that far off for some of them. But there are a few brighter bulbs among the dim ones so that helps."

Jason took another pull on his beer and glanced over at Rachel. "So what about you? Where are you from?"

"Here," she said with a shrug. "I've lived her all my life. I've never been anywhere else."

"What? Nowhere?" He leaned up on the arm of the chair. "How about vacations? Didn't your family go anywhere on a trip or something?"

"Nope, my dad managed a convenience store before he retired. We never went much anywhere. Wait, that's wrong, when I was in ninth grade my parents took me to Washington, D.C. I did really great on a government test so as a reward they took me and my sister up to see the capitol building for the weekend."

She sat back a moment and reflected on that trip with a simple smile on her face.

He settled back into his seat. "Have you ever been on a airplane?"

"Nope, someday I will."

Jason paused a moment. Rachel glanced over and could see from the expression on his face that he was cooking up something.

"Okay, here's the deal," he started with a gleam in his eye. "In three weeks I've got fall break at the college and we, you and I, are going to the Bahamas."

"What?"

"You heard me, I'm going to book us a flight and

hotel package tonight, it's off season down there now so it's the perfect time to go. I'll get two rooms adjoining but that won't matter because we'll spend most of the time on the beach anyway."

"Jason!"

"What? Don't you want to go?"

"Of course I want to go, but Jason," she replied looking a bit shocked, "I hardly know you. I mean we just met a couple of days ago for God's sake."

"It's not like we'll be sleeping together or anything. We'll have separate rooms. We're just two friends spending a couple of days in the Bahamas enjoying the beach. Or if you rather, we could drive somewhere and go to a museum or something. I just thought it would be great to fly somewhere close. They have these great weekend packages to the Bahamas…"

"Okay, I understand," she said interrupting. "It was just so sudden it took me by surprise."

She paused a moment and looked at Jason's eager face. Why did she want to do this so badly? He just made her feel so happy to be with him.

"So do you want to go with me to the Bahamas or would you prefer a museum or something? Your choice."

"The Bahamas," she whispered blushing a deep crimson.

"Cool. I'll get my laptop and we can book it together, right now."

They spent the rest of the evening haggling over room and airfare prices, but in the end they found a quaint little hotel off the beaten path that the website claimed had exceptional views and a short walk to the beach.

The next morning Jason walked out of his front door and turned to lock it as Rachel, dressed in pants and a jacket again, walked out into the hallway.

He turned and extended his hand. "Hi, we haven't formally met but I've spoken to your roommate a couple of times," Jason added with a huge grin.

"Hi, I'm Ray," he replied with a twinkle in his eye.

"It's nice to meet you Ray, I'm Jason," he replied. "Have a good day at work."

"Thanks, the same to you." He locked the apartment door and started down the stairs.

Jason had a late afternoon class that day so when he finally returned home he found an ice tea glass sitting on his kitchen counter with a small note beneath it. 'Hi, there was a network crash at work this afternoon so I had to go back and fix it before they wet their pants. Here's the glass I borrowed, see you Saturday night.'

=TWO=

The rest of the week whisked by in a flash and Jason soon found himself standing outside of Rachel's door pressing her doorbell.

She opened the door a moment later and smiled broadly. She stood there in a stunning sapphire blue dress that hugged her curves nicely. It was cut just above her knees and revealed just enough cleavage to make him want to dwell there more than he should.

She walked briskly back into her apartment in stocking feet. "I'll be just a minute. I just have to find a decent pair of shoes."

"You could try that pair of white sandals," he replied with a smirk. "I'm told they go with just about anything."

Rachel leaned back around the corner and raised an eyebrow. "I think I will." She scrunched her nose and smiled.

Several minutes later they walked out of the front door of the apartment building towards the parking lot.

Jason looked around the parking lot. "Would you like to drive or would you like me to?"

"I don't have a car so I guess it's up to you."

"Really? How do you get to work?"

"I take the bus. It's a direct route and thirty minutes later I'm dropped off nearly at my office door. Sometimes getting home can be a pain but most of the times it works out okay."

Jason opened the passenger door for her and she slid into the seat. He walked around his car and got in behind the wheel.

"Where are we going?" she asked with a curious smile.

"Not far. Do you like Indian food?"

"I've never had it, is it good?"

"My dear, you are in for a treat."

Twenty minutes later they walked into the Taj Mahal, a local restaurant that specialized in southern Indian cuisine. "The smells are so intoxicating," she murmured softly as they followed the waiter to their table. She glanced around as she walked. "It so exotic in here."

"I can't believe that you've never been in an Indian restaurant," he said as they both sat down in one of the booths.

"That's me, I'm an Indian food virgin. So what should I order?" She picked up the menu "I have no idea what I'm looking at."

"Don't worry, we'll get the sample platter for two. It's the best way to discover everything. Sometimes the stuff can be terribly hot but I'll steer you clear of those items if you're palate isn't used to spicy hot foods.

After they ordered dinner and the waiter left

their table, Rachel looked up and smiled at Jason. "Thank you for not making a fuss the other morning in the hallway."

"Why would you expect me to do something like that?"

"Because so many people would." Then she spoke as if she was making the discovery as she was speaking the words. "But you're not like that, are you?"

She glanced at Jason with a sweet smile. Then she narrowed her eyes. They sparkled with a fiery intensity.

"You let me paint your toenails didn't you," she whispered as she smacked his arm playfully. "You knew what I was doing the whole time and you just laid there and played possum, didn't you?"

Jason blushed a bit and grinned sheepishly.

Rachel leaned back against the back of the booth and sighed. "Are you playing with me?"

"Never."

"I have no idea who you are," she said looking at him with a renewed sense of wonder.

"I feel the same way," he replied sipping his wine. "Someone wise once said that half the fun in life is the journey of discovery."

Rachel sat a moment and looked into Jason's eyes. "How lucky for the two of us to be sharing a terrace."

"I don't believe in luck. Kismet yes, but never luck."

"Kismet?"

He nodded then took a sip of his water. "Meant to be. It's Arabic or Turkish, or something like that. When something is meant to be it's said to be

Kismet."

"Oh," she said quietly lost in thought.

"Do you care to explain what I saw the other day in the hallway? I don't suppose you are a cross-dresser too, are you?"

"It's not really cross-dressing. I'm just following my instincts."

"Huh?"

Rachel smiled at the perplexed look on his face. "I can't believe I'm going to tell you this. God, I only met you a week ago and now here I sit ready to spill my whole life story. You must think I some sort of a ditz."

"Hardly," he said softly and she looked at him quizzically. "In the short time that I've known you I find you totally captivating, Rachel. You're funny, and smart and you can hold an intelligent conversation, which is more than I can say for some of my students and colleagues at school."

He paused a moment to dab his mouth with a napkin. "I know this will sound a bit forward, but knowing there's a chance we might bump into one another with the likelihood that it will lead to another entertaining conversation makes coming home all the more enjoyable."

He blushed a bit and dropped his eyes. "I suppose I went too far with that last line but I do mean it," he continued in a hushed tone as he glanced back up to her. "I look forward to our conversations on the terrace even if I do get my toenails painted red from time to time."

Rachel paused a moment and just stared at Jason. He began blushing brighter under the intensity of her beautiful blue eyes.

"Did I say too much?"

"Huh? Ah, no. God, I'm sorry, I just sort of blanked there, like my brain froze and I needed to reboot." Rachel blushed crimson and looked away a moment.

She glanced sideways at him and smiled. "Jason, I like our conversations too. They're just quirky enough to keep me totally enthralled and I love it. So, no, you didn't say too much. Perhaps I'm the one who's not saying enough. Anyway, here goes, I'm taking the plunge once again."

She shifted in her seat and sipped her wine a second as she collected her thoughts. She was about to begin when she stopped and looked at Jason carefully. "I need to ask you something first. I've told people who I thought would understand my little secret and I've been burnt more times than I want to remember."

Jason sat quietly as she worked through her thoughts out loud. "But then…you shared a secret with me the first day we met, didn't you?" She was finding herself once again on a path of discovery about him. "So I suppose it's only fair of me to share one with you. Can you keep a secret?"

Jason nodded. "If you ask me I'll keep it forever."

Rachel smiled and reached across the table to touch his hand. About then, the waiter arrived with their food. He sat platter after platter on the table and before long, it was filled an amazing assortment of delights. Each dish gave off a remarkable aroma that swirled together and delicately teased her nose.

"Enjoy, Rachel," he said as he breathed in deeply. "We can share stories later."

The rest of the meal was filled with the sighs and moans of pleasure as Rachel's palate discovered the exotic world of richly spiced but not necessarily hot Indian food. The richness of the flavor and the lush aromas kept the conversation to a minimum throughout the dinner.

"Oh my," she said gushing a bit, "I've just fallen in love with Indian cuisine! We have to come back here again, real soon."

"It would be my pleasure," Jason replied with a broad smile.

An hour later they left the restaurant and Jason drove down towards the river that meandered through the city. There was a walk that followed the riverbank. It eventually led them to one of the city parks that connected to the river walk. They found a set of swings in a play area nearby and Rachel sat in one as Jason joined her in another.

"It's crazy and I can't explain it, but I feel like I've known you all my life." She rocked gently back and forth.

"I know, Kismet."

"Yeah, Kismet."

They swung silently for a while, listening to the night sounds along the river. "This has never happened to me either," Jason finally admitted. "Usually, when I meet a girl, I stumble awkwardly like some schoolboy on his first date. It's really is pathetic to watch. But you're just so easy to talk to.

"Yes, so are you."

She rummaged around in her purse and found her cellphone. A few clicks brought it to life and she opened up a browser window. "Here," she said as she handed him her phone, "I'm what you call an intersexed person, I Googled it for you. Click the first link."

Jason studied the page for a few minutes and then, with a curious smile on his face, he handed it back to her.

"Thanks, this explains a few things."

"Are you grossed out?" A look of worry filled her face.

"No. Not in the least. Fascinated, enchanted, but never grossed out. Life is too fantastic to ever be grossed out about something like that."

"I was right," she said, beaming at him, "you are unique."

"But how does this explain what I saw Wednesday morning in the hallway?"

"Ah, well," she paused for a moment while she collected her thoughts again and pressed on. "In the legal world I've found that some people are rather narrow-minded in their viewpoint on life. Not all of them, but it's been my experience that there are a lot more of them than you'd expect."

"If I showed up in a skirt and blouse to do what I do, I would become an object not a person. In their mind girls don't do IT work, only guys do. In slacks, a shirt, and the occasional tie, I can go about my day fixing their little boo-boos and nobody even looks twice at me. I'm the IT guy. They pay me very well to blend into the woodwork and not be a distraction."

"Yes, but what about the women in the firm? I mean, come on, you do make a rather handsome young man, even with a hint of mascara in the corners of your eyes."

"What? You saw that?" She smacked him again

playfully on the arm. "Why didn't you say something?"

"Because, if I did, you'd have been mortified and we wouldn't be having this conversation right now, would we?"

She blushed crimson and turned away to look out over the river. "I suppose you're right. Stupid social construct," she fumed quietly.

"Absolutely. Hey, we should have t-shirts with that printed on them."

"And they both should be tie-dyed in pink an blue!"

They fell into fits of laughter holding on to one another to keep from falling out of the swings. In a moment, the laughter was gone and replaced by the silence of reflection as they retreated into their own thoughts. She looked over at Jason and smiled warmly and he returned her smile.

"So do you date women or men?"

She blushed slightly. "I've been with both but I'm really attracted to men."

"Oh."

They sat in awkward silence a while longer and watched the river lap against the bank.

"I suppose we should go, before the drunks take over the park and kick us out."

As they strolled back to Jason's car they walked close to each other, hand in hand. He had a blissful smile on his face and she leaned her head to rest it on his shoulder as they walked.

The drive home was quiet and serene. 'Kismet' was a word that seemed to meander through his mind. Meant to be.

In the hallway outside of their apartments, Jason

led her up to her door and kissed her cheek. "Thank you, Rachel."

"That was a lovely dinner followed by a delightful evening," she replied softly.

"I'd like to do that again sometime."

"Me too. How about we stay in and I cook up something next Friday?"

"I'm looking forward to it. Oh, and Rachel…"

"Yes?"

"You don't have to have an excuse to visit. The terrace door is always open."

She smiled and as she opened her apartment door she blew him a kiss. "Mine too. "Good night, Jason," she said as she stepped inside.

"Good night Rachel," he replied and walked into his apartment.

=THREE=

The next morning Jason walked out onto the terrace with the Sunday paper and a steaming hot cup of coffee in his hands. He plunked down on his wicker chaise lounge and leaned back to enjoy the early morning tranquility. He heard Rachel's screen door slide open and he heard her step out on to the terrace.

"A cup of coffee and the paper to start your day?"

"Can I come around?" She stood near the low wall in her bathrobe and nightgown. "I'm not really dressed for scaling walls."

"Absolutely, I'll unlock the front door."

A few minutes later she was comfortably wrapped in her robe and slippers sipping on a cup of coffee, with her nose buried in the weekend section of the paper. "This is nice," she sighed as she looked up a moment and caught him glancing at her.

"Thanks, but I can't take all the credit. Sundays are my favorite day of the week. I rush around like a madman all day Saturday to finish my homework and chores so that I can just relax and spend the day decompressing."

"I forgot to ask last night, how was your first few days of school?"

"Hectic, and frenetic, with a pinch of crazy."

"That doesn't sound like much fun."

"It'll get better, the week leading up to classes is always nuts. How are things in the world of 'it'?"

She laughed and reached over to smack him on the arm playfully with the newspaper. "Fine, totally crazy too."

They talked about his classes and the dummies in her office like they were old friends. There was a sense of comfort between the two of them, as if they were childhood friends who've been separated for a long time and were now finally trying to catch up.

After a while, they sat quiet for a moment and idly watched the world drift by.

Eventually, with a gleam in her eye, Rachel leaned over and whispered seductively in Jason's ear. "You want to play dress-up?"

"What?" His face flushed red.

"You heard me," she replied with a devilish smile. "Come on, you don't have a single thing planned today. You told me so a minute ago. And I want to see you in heels again."

"I do not make a good looking woman," he replied very emphatically.

She looked at him askance and he balked a moment.

"I don't…honestly. I'm sure you've seen those strange looking hairy men in panty hose and heels on the Internet. It's grotesque. I don't want any part of it."

"But you've done it before, you said so the first time we met."

"Yes, but that was in private. Plus it was well lubricated with alcohol. I took one look at myself in the mirror and swore I'd never do it again."

"But you did, didn't you?"

"Yes, but only once more and that was to prove to myself that I still looked ridiculous, and I did. Besides, I could never do it in front of you. I'd be too embarrassed."

"Let me dress you."

"No."

"You can wear the sandals again."

He paused a moment then shook his head. "No."

"All right, how about, just as a test, you let me do your hair and makeup? If, after I'm through, you aren't completely convinced that you're attractive as a woman I'll never ask you to do it again, ever."

"Is that a promise?"

"Yes, I promise," she replied holding her fingers crossed behind her back.

And of course, she proved him wrong.

Forty minutes later Jason stood awe-struck in front of the full-length mirror in her bathroom. He couldn't believe what he was seeing. What was reflected back was a really pretty woman.

"You are a magician," he murmured softly.

"Thank you," Rachel replied as she kissed him on the cheek. "All I did was do a little enhancing. You already have really nice features. And even though your hair is short I was able to do something perky and cute."

"Why did you want to do this?"

"Because sometimes it's nice to talk to a girlfriend."

"But…"

"Look in that mirror and tell me you don't see a beautiful woman," she said tilting his face towards the mirror.

Jason had to admit, he did look like a woman. It was uncanny.

"Besides, ever since I saw you walk in my sandals I've wanted to get you into a dress so we could go shopping."

"Oh no, I'm not leaving the apartment. That was not part of the deal."

"I know sweetie but you look so good and I really do need to buy a new pair of shoes for work." She pleaded with a little girl pout. "I want to go shopping with my new girlfriend. Besides, you're the one with the car."

"You don't play fair."

"Never," she replied tracing her finger across his chin with a wicked smile. "I like to get my way."

He sat for a minute and considered her request. The longer he sat the more doubt colored her expression.

"Okay, I'll go shopping with you," he said reluctantly and her eyes began to sparkle again. "But on one condition."

"And that is?" she asked looking skeptical.

"It doesn't happen in a dress. I'm wearing jeans and a t-shirt," he insisted with a stern expression that told her he wasn't going to budge on this issue.

"Agreed," she said quickly which worried Jason that somehow he'd missed an important point in their negotiation.

Rachel rummaged around in her closet and pulled out a pair of ballet flats. "Here, wear these."

He opened his mouth to protest but she interrupted him.

"Or do you want everyone to see your red toenails with your flip-flops?"

He looked down at his feet with a cockeyed grin. "Okay, but no more negotiations," he added wagging his finger at her.

She leaned forward and kissed his wagging fingertip. "Deal."

Jason pulled his car out of the building parking lot and turned towards the downtown mall. "I assume we're going to the mall?"

"Nope, turn right at the light. We're going to the Shoe Boutique on 29th and Grove Street. My friend Sandra runs the place and I shop there a lot."

"This isn't an attempt to tease me because I played possum is it?"

"No silly," she replied with a wicked grin. "That comes later."

Jason groaned and she giggled.

The Shoe Boutique was one of those trendy shoe warehouse places where a girl could find almost any shoe from innocent to decadent in almost any color and size. Jason parked his car in the parking lot in front of the building and turned off the engine.

"I think you need a new name," she mused casually. "I can't just call my new girlfriend Jason after all."

Jason thought for a moment and then he turned

to Rachel with a wistful smile. "You can call me Jessica, or Jessie."

"I like it, but why did you pick that name?"

"That was my twin sister's name. She died when I was only seven."

She sat looking down at her hands. "She got meningitis at school and she was gone before I even knew what happened."

"I'm so sorry," Rachel whispered as she reached over to place her hand over Jason's, now Jessie's hands.

"No, it's okay," she looked up quickly and smiled. "If I take her name it's as if she still lives on in me. I like that a little bit of Jessie is still with me."

"Come on, Jess," Rachel said taking a big breath to settle her emotions, "let's go buy some shoes."

When they got out of his car Jessie looked apprehensively at Rachel.

"Oh don't worry, you look lovely," she said encouragingly. "And besides nobody cares and if they do it's their problem not ours."

"Thanks."

"But you do need to get your ears pierced," she said as she strode towards the shoe store.

"Huh-eh," he groaned as he stood in the middle of the parking lot, "that wasn't part of the deal!"

Rachel turned and waved impishly and then disappeared inside the store and beyond earshot.

As Jason walked into the boutique he began to understand why women had so many shoes.

"My God there are so many," he whispered once he caught up with Rachel.

"I know, isn't it divine?"

"What are you looking for?" She looked around

hoping she wasn't drawing the wrong kind of attention.

"Some new flats and a pair of oxfords for work," Rachel replied preoccupied with an elegant pair of platform pumps that, although fairly simple, looked very stylish.

"Hmm, none my size," she said disappointed as she replaced the pumps on the shelf.

Rachel walked further down the aisle and pulled a pair of red spiked heels off the shelf. She turned and handed them to Jessie.

"Here, try these on, they're your size." She stood watching her with a gleam in her eye. "I like the fact that my new girlfriend wears the same shoe size as me. That way we can share." She giggled and pushed the shoes into Jessie's hands.

"I can't, not here," she hissed softly.

"Of course you can. Just look at them, they're gorgeous and you know you want to put them on. I can see it in your eyes."

Jessie blushed brightly and looked around the store to see if anyone else was watching. Fortunately, on a Sunday morning, the store was mostly empty so he glanced back to Rachel and saw her reassuring smile.

"Okay," she whispered.

Rachel smiled like a the cat who just caught the mouse as Jessie took off the ballet flats and slipped her feet into the luxury of a five-inch pair of stilettos that fit like a glove. They were fire engine red with an ankle strap and a lace vamp. And from the look on her face they were also 'sold'.

It was obvious to anyone who paid the least bit of attention to the the girl in the red shoes that she had a thing for heels.

While Rachel browsed through the oxfords, Jessie wandered up and down every aisle trying on pair after pair. She walked in those new shoes like they were made for her. A few minutes later Rachel found her looking at the clearance rack.

"Hey Jess, what did you find?"

"Look at these," she gushed with a gleam in her eye. "They're marked down too."

"They're still too much," Rachel replied, "and look, the stitching is not that great. Besides, the red ones you are wearing are way nicer for more than half as much as the markdown."

Jessie looked at the shoes again then sat them back on the shelf with a huff. She turned and followed Rachel to the checkout counter a bit disappointed but at the same time Rachel was right.

"Is Sarah here?" Rachel asked the clerk at the sales register.

The sales clerk shook her head. "Not today, she's on a buying trip up north."

"Oh well, we'll take these," she said pulling out her credit card. "I think she'll wear those out, too."

Jessie blushed slightly and handed the clerk the shoebox that her heels came in filled with the ballet flats.

Several minutes later, with shoeboxes in hand, they made their way across the parking lot and back to his car. She loved the clicking sound her heels made on the parking lot pavement.

"That was so much fun!" she said as she slipped in behind the steering wheel. "Thank you Rachel!"

"Thank you, Jessie," Rachel replied. "I haven't had that much fun shopping in ages. You went a little crazy in there you know."

"Yes, thank you for being the voice of reason," she replied. "I nearly blew a month's rent. I guess I got a little excited."

"A little? I can't imagine how you'll react when we go to Victoria's Secret." Rachel mused.

"No, it's just shoes," he murmured. "I love high heeled shoes. Ever since I was a little kid I've always admired my mother's shoes. The rest of women's lingerie is, well, I've never felt the need."

She didn't want to take off the heels but when it became obvious that she might wreck the car if he drove in them, she relented. Jessie started the car and pulled out of the parking lot to head back to the apartment building.

A couple of blocks away she pulled up to the stoplight at the intersection and looked over at Rachel.

"So thanks again for today." She smiled blissfully. "It was really special."

Rachel's eyes sparkled in the late afternoon sunlight. "Can we stop for some groceries on the way back?" she asked.

"Sure."

It was getting dark as they climbed the three flights of stairs to their front doors. They were both laden with shoeboxes and grocery bags.

Jessie looked at Rachel and smiled sweetly. "I don't know how women do it. Three flights of stairs in five-inch heels, this is totally dangerous."

"I know, that's why I've never tried it," Rachel giggled.

"I guess I'm still caught up in the moment. Remind me how dumb this is the next time I attempt it."

"Will there be a next time?"

"Probably," she smirked as Rachel opened her apartment door.

Jessie carried Rachel's groceries into her kitchen and set them on the counter.

Rachel opened her refrigerator and started to put a few things away. "How about we order pizza and sit out on the terrace?"

"Sounds great," Jessie replied. Let me get my stuff put away and I'll bring the beer."

Thirty minutes later they sat watching the trees sway in the evening breeze. Jessie had her new shoes propped up against the terrace rail, admiring them in the moonlight.

"We both have to work in the morning, don't we?" Rachel said as she reached across and touched Jessie's arm.

"Yeah, back to reality. I have my first class at nine tomorrow and my first night class as well," she replied with a sigh. "It's going to be a long day."

"What time do you have to leave in the morning?"

"Around eight I guess." She got up and carried the dishes into the kitchen. A moment later she came back to the terrace and stood near the low wall.

"I'll see you tomorrow morning." Jessie stepped over the wall to walk towards her terrace door.

"See you," Rachel said as she slid her door shut.

=FOUR=

The next morning was just like every other Monday morning, only this time Jason was loaded down with books. He juggled the pile precariously while trying to lock his door. At that moment Rachel stepped out into the hallway dressed as Ray.

She reached for Jason's pile of books. "Here, let me help you with that."

"Thanks, the first day of classes and already I'm overwhelmed."

Jason locked his door and took his pile of books back from Ray then they both turned and walked down the stairs towards the building parking lot.

"Have a good one," Ray said as she walked off towards the bus stop on the corner.

Jason opened his car trunk with the remote and deposited the books in the corner of this trunk. He turned to see Ray board the bus. He thought again about his shopping trip yesterday and smiled. Then he got into his car and drove off towards the college.

That night he didn't get in until after ten so he

knew that she was probably already in bed. He dropped his book bag near the couch then, exhausted, he walked slowly across the room towards his bedroom.

He looked at the shoebox sitting on the chair by his closet. The red heels shimmered in the light from the hallway. He wanted to put them on but he resisted the urge. He decided to wait until the next time he was with Rachel. He quickly got undressed and slipped quietly into bed. Moments later he was asleep.

The next morning, feeling a lot better, he stood waiting for Ray to come out of her door. He wanted to thank her again for helping out yesterday and to ask her if her 'roommate' was up for drinks after work in the afternoon. But Ray was late. In fact, it was nearly nine-thirty and she still hadn't opened the door.

Jason knocked on Rachel's door and waited but she didn't answer.

Maybe she had to leave early. He shrugged his shoulders and walked off down the stairs towards his car.

Inside her bedroom, Rachel laid in her bed curled up into a tiny ball. The aspirin was just beginning to wear off again. She reached over and opened the bottle to get two more pills.

The swelling around her eyes and lips throbbed as she popped the pills in her mouth and swallowed a bit of the tepid water from the cup on the nightstand. Her body ached all over. The bandages that the emergency room nurse put on her pulled against her skin uncomfortably.

She heard Jason knock on her front door but she didn't want to see him right now. She didn't want to see anyone. She closed her eyes and tried to will the pain away.

She reached up and felt the swelling around her eyes. She was too afraid to get up and pull the bandages away to look at the damage the asshole inflicted on her last night. She sank back into her pillow with the hope that sleep would turn it all into a bad dream.

=FIVE=

Jason came home in the afternoon and stopped inside the apartment building foyer. He noticed that there were several letters still stuffed in Rachel's mailbox.

When he climbed the last of the three flights of stairs to his apartment he saw that Rachel's paper was still outside her door. That was odd. She always takes it with her when she goes to work.

Deep inside his chest he was beginning to feel uneasy. Jason opened his door and dropped his book bag near the kitchen counter. He pulled out his cellphone, and then he remembered that neither of them had shared their phone numbers yet.

Jason set his phone on the kitchen counter and walked briskly out the terrace door. He hopped over the low wall that separated the two apartment terraces and slid open Rachel's terrace door.

When he pushed back the drapery that covered her door the afternoon light flooded the darkened room. His uneasiness continued to grow.

"Rachel?" He called out softly, "are you in here?"

"Jason?" He heard her weak voice coming from her bedroom.

"Yeah, are you all right?" He walked down the hallway that led to her bedroom. "I saw the newspaper outside of your door and...well, I wanted to see if you're okay." Jason stepped up to her bedroom door and pushed it open gently. Inside he saw her lying on her bed with an icepack on her face. It barely covered the swelling that was evident even in the darkness of her bedroom.

"Holy shit! What happened?" He raced around the bed to kneel close to her.

Rachel began to cry as he knelt down next to her. "Jason, please I'm not dealing with things very well right now." Her sobbing made it difficult to understand what she was saying.

"Is there anything I can do, anything?"

"Not now. Just go Jason. I'll be fine, just go, okay? I'll see you tomorrow, okay?"

Jason stood up slowly and walked to her bedroom door. He looked back at her; his face was filled with worry. "Would you like to talk to Jessie?" he asked in a quiet whisper and Rachel stopped crying for a moment.

She pulled back the icepack from her eyes and looked at Jason. She nodded meekly and Jason smiled. "Okay."

Thirty minutes later Rachel heard the click of Jessie's heels on the terrace floor outside of her apartment. A moment later Jessie stood at her bedroom door and peeked in.

"Hey there sweetie, how are you doing?" Jessie

walked over to Rachel's bed and sat down gently next to her. She wrapped her arms around Rachel's shoulders and smoothed her hair, tucking a lock behind her ear. She collapsed against Jessie as her eyes filled with tears.

Jessie held her a moment and let her release all the emotions and pain that had been bottled up inside her since she was beaten. Her sobs began to subside and she wiped her nose with a tissue.

"What happened?"

"I came home early Monday," she sniffled, "and I knew you were going to be late with a night class so I decided to shop for some more groceries for Friday. I was almost out the door when I got a call from an old friend of mine. They were going to a club downtown and they wanted to know if I would join them. I thought, 'what the heck,' and decided to indulge myself. They only knew me as Rachel so I changed clothes and headed out to meet them."

Rachel snuggled against Jessie's chest and continued with her story as she pulled her arm around her chest.

"Things were going along fine; everybody was having a great time. It was so nice to catch up and all. A little later a bunch of guys stopped by and started hitting on us. I was flattered and thought it wouldn't be any big deal to do a little flirting. This guy, Bob, started to get a little too aggressive so I decided to let things cool off and go to the bathroom."

Rachel was beginning to get more agitated so Jessie began to calmly stroke her hair.

"But when I walked out of the stall he was in the women's bathroom. He started getting really forceful. I tried to push him off but he was a lot bigger than me and he pressed me against the wall. He kept telling me how beautiful I was and that he wasn't going to hurt me. I struggled against him but he was so damn big. Then, when his hand slipped between my legs he felt something that surprised him. He called me a filthy fagot and he went ballistic."

"Let me see what he did." Jessie tilted her face up into the light. It was swollen around the eye socket and along the bridge of her nose but it didn't look like he damaged her eyes. The bruising made it hard to determine if the bastard broke her nose.

She had some scrapes and scratches on her lips and throat that looked like they needed some attention as well. She looked rough but it could have been worse. Jessie kissed her forehead. It was clear that she needed to see aspecialist more than an emergency room patch up.

"Come on, girl, let's get you up." She lifted Rachel up. "I'm going to take you to the doctor. It doesn't look that bad but I'm no medical expert so you should have this looked at to be safe."

"I don't want to go out looking like this, Jessie." She resisted Jessie's pull.

"I know, sweetheart, but I would never forgive myself if this turned into something bad so come on," she said determinedly, "I insist."

"What am I going to do about work?" Rachel looked a bit worried in spite of the bruises on her face.

"We'll deal with that later," Jessie replied slipping on Rachel's shoes and pulling her out of her bed.

They stopped at Jessie's apartment while she took off the red heels she wore to visit and put on a pair of running shoes. She blushed a bit at Rachel as she closed the apartment door. "I still can't drive in heels," she mumbled as they walked towards the stairs.

Two hours later they walked out of the clinic with a handful of painkillers and some salve. Rachel took three stitches in her lip and there were multiple dressings on the scrapes and cuts along her neck and cheeks. When they got back to the apartment Jessie helped her to her couch.

"Is there someone from work that you can call?"

"My supervisor," Rachel said picking up her phone and dialing. "Hello, Oscar? Yeah, it's me Ray. I was in a bit of an accident. No, I'm all right. I'm just a little banged up. My friend Jessie is taking care of me right now. Yeah. Anyway, I won't be in until this heals up. Hopefully, it will be only a day or two. Right, okay, I'll call you when I'm better. Okay, bye."

She clipped her cellphone shut and smiled bleakly at Jessie. "You still have mascara and shadow on, you know that?" She asked placing her hand on Jessie's cheek.

"I didn't do a very good job to begin with so the doctor probably thought we just came from a 'Goth' party," she said with a chuckle.

"What, at seven in the evening? You're very silly Jessie, but thank you." Her smile was beautiful even though it had to hurt to smile right now.

"While you have your cellphone out, let me dial this number," she said opening up her phone and punching in his cell number. She could faintly hear the cellphone ringing in the next apartment.

Jessie let it wring a moment then stopped the call. "It's my phone," she said. "I didn't have your number today or I would have called first. But then," she said slowly realizing what that meant, "if I did have it you would never have let me see you like this, would you?"

Rachel blushed a bit and dropped her eyes. "Will you stay with me for a while?"

"Sure, we'll get carryout and we can watch silly movies all night." Jessie sat next to her and pulled her into a gentle hug.

"I'd like that very much," Rachel whispered.

It wasn't long after the pizza was delivered that the painkillers began to really kick in and Rachel fell asleep nuzzled against Jessie's arm. She turned the television off and brought some blankets from the bedroom. Jessie tucked her in and kissed her on top of her head. Then she tiptoed out the terrace door and back into her apartment.

The next morning Jason called his department secretary at the college and asked her to send a note to all his students telling them that he would not be in today. He rummaged around in his refrigerator and pulled out what he needed and set it in a pile on the counter.

He grabbed his cellphone and headed back to Rachel's to cook her breakfast. A few minutes after the aroma of bacon began to fill the air Rachel leaned up on the back of the couch and looked over to see him busy in the kitchen.

She got up slowly and walked into the kitchen. Without a word she wrapped her arms around him and kissed him on the nape of his neck. She smiled gently then she turned and walked slowly to the bathroom.

A minute later Jason heard the shower start. When she returned her hair was wrapped in a towel and she carried her first aide kit with some of the dressings that the doctor had given her. Jason helped her redress her wounds.

She was looking better. The swelling was beginning to go down a little and the discoloration was shifting towards black and blue. He knew all of this would take a while to get back to normal but he was glad that she was on the mend and that nothing that asshole did to her was permanent.

After breakfast Rachel took Jason by the arm and pulled him over to the couch. "I need to talk to you about Jessie," she said shyly. "I know it's a bit strange but I like that side of you. Not more than you but," she struggled a moment to find the right words. "There are things that I feel like I can tell Jessie that I would be way too embarrassed to tell you. I know you must think I'm weird but..."

"It's okay," he interrupted her gently. "I understand, kind of. I mean if you think about it, there are things that I can do with Ray that I could never do with you too."

"Like what?"

"Well go into the men's bathroom and pee standing up for instance," he replied with a broad grin.

Rachel blushed profusely and playfully smacked him on the arm again. Then she leaned forward and kissed him gently on the lips. Jason held her shoulders and leaned back to look into her dazzling eyes. She sat there a moment with an impish smile.

"What?" she asked coyly.

"Nothing. I was just thinking how glad I am that you like to paint your neighbor's toenails red."

He released her and she fell back into his arms to

snuggle there for the rest of the day.

The next morning Jason waited outside of her apartment. She walked out her door dressed as Ray and smiled shyly at him.

"You know this is only going to solidify their resolve that you a definitely a guy, don't you?" he smirked looking to see if her shiner had further reduced its swelling.

"Shut up," she grinned as she smacked his arm playfully. "Next time I'll just scratch and spit if I want to rack up some man points. Are you giving me a ride or what?"

"No problem, dude," he said with a big grin as they both walked down the stairs hand in hand.

=SIX=

"Hanna, guess what? I just got a promotion!" Rachel almost shouted into her phone at her sister Hanna.

"It's about time," Hanna replied eagerly. "Now you can move out of that dump you call an apartment and find someplace nice."

"Umm, not yet," Rachel replied sounding rather coquettish. "So tell me, what's happening in your life? We haven't talked in ages."

Hanna told Rachel about her daughter's recital and her husband Bob's latest 'fly-by-night' hobby venture.

"He's into model rockets now." If Rachel could see her sister she knew she must have been rolling her eyes. That was one of Hanna's favorite things to do.

"So tell me," Hanna asked with more than a hint of curiosity, "what's keeping you at 'Maison Hole-in-the-Wall' anyway? You totally dodged the question earlier."

"Well, eh, I've met someone recently and, well,

he's totally nice," Rachel stammered a bit and then everything went quiet. Hanna was totally silent on the other end.

"Does he know about you?"

"Yeah."

"Really?" Hanna's voice was laced with worry. "Little sister, you're such an incurable romantic, are you really sure? I don't know if I can take another crash and burn like the last time."

"No, Hanna, this is different, way different. I got pretty banged up a few weeks ago and he was totally there for me."

"Banged up? How?" Hanna demanded.

"This random guy in a bar. I was out with some friends I hadn't seen in years and this creep started hitting on me. The next thing I knew he shoved his hand up my skirt and then he started beating me."

"My God Rachel, that's called assault! Did you get his name? Are you going to press charges? "

"It all happened so fast and then he was gone. I never saw him again and I probably never will. If he ever does show up again it'll be all I can do to keep Jason from killing him."

"Jason? That's his name, your neighbor who helped you?"

Rachel could hear the mounting concern in her voice. "Yes, his name is Jason. He's so gracious and kind. He even likes a lot of the same things that I do."

An image of Jessie flashed into Rachel's mind. It was followed quickly by thoughts of her and Jessie buying shoes. She thought about telling Hanna about Jessie, Jason's female counterpart, but decided that it needed to stay a secret between just her and Jason for now, perhaps forever. The thought of forever brought a subtle smile to her face.

Rachel drifted back from her reverie to the conversation as her sister finished telling her how happy she is for Rachel and that she would really like to meet him.

"Huh?" Rachel recovered from her reverie. "Oh sure, I'll talk to him later today, perhaps we can meet over coffee this weekend."

Rachel heard a thump that could only mean that Jason's home. She glanced over at the new bottle of red wine she bought to celebrate. She walked to the kitchen and found her corkscrew and two glasses.

"Sis, I have to go. I'll call you tomorrow if we can make it for coffee on Saturday, okay?"

"Sure thing Rachel, wait, I have a hectic Saturday but Sunday looks wide open," she replied sounding excited.

"Okay, bye."

She closed her phone and picked up the wine bottle as she walked towards the terrace door.

Rachel stepped over the low fence on the terrace balancing a bottle of wine, a corkscrew, and two glasses. She was anxious to see Jason and tell him the good news. As she passed by the kitchen window she glanced in and saw a woman sitting on the couch with Jason. She stopped in her tracks.

The woman in Jason's apartment was beautiful. She had long flowing hair that fell in luscious curls across her shoulders. She had high cheekbones and well-defined eyebrows that framed lovely eyes and a radiant smile. From the way she was acting she must have known Jason before, perhaps intimately.

Rachel watched the woman reach across the

distance to lay her hand gently on his arm. The smile on her face told it all and Rachel's heart began to twist up inside.

Once again the pain of disappointment reared its ugly head. She could hear laughter coming from his apartment but she couldn't make out what they were saying. She inched closer to the window.

Rachel turned and looked at the trees swaying in the late afternoon sun then she looked down at her bottle of wine. Her eyes began to glisten.

She was heartsick. The woman must be an old girlfriend. Jason might be getting back together with her. She heard more laughter and then she heard the woman say, "Please come back to Cleveland with me Jason, we all miss you so very much up there."

"I miss you too," she heard Jason reply to the woman on the couch.

Rachel closed her eyes tightly and tried to squeeze out the pain. She turned and stepped quietly over the low fence that separated Jason's side of the terrace from hers and ran back into her apartment.

Suddenly her phone began to ring. She walked over to the kitchen counter and picked it up. It was Jason calling her. She pushed the mute button and set it down. She couldn't face him, not now anyway. She buried her face in a pillow and just sobbed.

=SEVEN=

It was nearly nine o'clock the following morning and Rachel was nowhere to be seen. Jason started to worry. He tapped at her door but she didn't answer. He looked down and noticed that the newspaper was gone. That meant that she'd gone out already.

She must have had to leave early. Crisis in the land of 'it' no doubt.

That evening when he returned home, he knocked gently on her door. She didn't respond. He listened quietly but everything was silent. He shrugged his shoulders thinking that she must have gone out with friends for the evening.

The next day as Jason stood in the hallway locking his door, he watched as Rachel, dressed as Ray, came out and locked her door. "Good morning," he said cheerfully.

She glanced at him briefly then she hid her face with her ball cap and quickly ran off down the stairs.

"Hey Ray, what's going on? Are you all right?" Jason shouted but Ray just continued down the stairs and out into the parking lot running as fast as she could.

All morning long he tried calling her but she never picked up. Finally, it was time for his first class of the day. Jason closed his office door and walked down the building corridor. His face couldn't hide his growing concern that Rachel was acting strangely all of a sudden. It was as if she didn't want to talk to him.

His thoughts were filled with worry. Did he do something wrong? What did he do? He kept playing the thoughts through his mind for the rest of the day.

That evening after he returned from work, he hopped over the dividing wall and walked to her terrace door. He tried to open it but it was locked.

It was never locked.

Now he really began to worry. She was shutting him out of her life. But, why? Dejected, he turned and walked slowly back to his apartment. Why was she avoiding him? He didn't understand it! He tried to call her again. This time he could hear her cellphone ring next door but still she didn't answer. He was really getting worried now.

Jason sat down on the couch and grabbed a piece of paper and pen from his briefcase. He started to write a letter then he scratched through a sentence and crumpled it up.

He pulled out another piece of paper and started again. 'Rachel, this is Jessie. I don't know what's going on but I need to see you. I'm waiting in the hallway, please let me in.'

After he finished the note he went into his bedroom to put on some makeup then he slipped on his red heels. He opened his front door and walked out into the hallway to stand in front of Rachel's door. He knelt down and slipped the note under her door.

A moment or two later the door slowly opened and Rachel looked at Jessie. Her eyes were red with crying but through her tears she could also see the hurt in Jessie's eyes. She opened the door further to let Jessie walk in.

"God, I was so scared that someone beat you up again," Jessie stammered as she turned and looked at her. "Are you all right? What's going on? Why won't you speak to me? Are you going to tell me why you've shut yourself up in here? Rachel…talk to me."

Rachel stood silently watching Jessie. She could see the hurt and disappointment filling her eyes. She wanted so badly to reach out and touch her, to hold her in her arms and help her ease the pain. Finally, she gathered her courage and looked Jessie in the eyes.

"I saw Jacob with a woman in his apartment. I was coming over with a bottle of wine to celebrate a promotion I got at work and I saw her in the kitchen window."

Rachel was sobbing now and it was hard for Jessie to make out what she was saying. "She was sitting on the couch with him and…well, it looked like they were going to kiss."

Jessie pulled her over to the couch.

Rachel sat down on the edge of the cushion trembling. "I couldn't help but overhear her tell him that she misses him terribly," she continued. "I heard her tell him that she wants him to come back to Cleveland. I heard him tell her that he misses her too.

I thought she was his ex-girlfriend or something. I panicked and ran back here. I couldn't face him. It hurt so much!"

"Rachel! That was Karen Rolands! She's my cousin! We went to high school together. She's married to a doctor and has two kids! They live in Cleveland. She and my grandma were the only ones on both sides of my whole fucked up family who supported me when I decided not to go into the military. Christ, she's like an older sister to me!"

"Oh." Rachel eyes were still brimming with tears. They trailed down her cheeks and dropped like tiny pearls to land carelessly in her lap. She leaned forward and fell against Jessie's chest sobbing.

Jessie's eyes began to tear up as well. She reached out and wrapped her arms around Rachel and gently hugged her.

"Rachel," Jessie began slowly but Rachel sat up and cut him off.

"Wait, I know Jessie," she said through sniffles, "I need to talk to Jason. I'm sorry."

"No, that's not it." Jessie paused a moment and took a big breath then let it out slowly. "I know this is going to sound schitzo-weird but the Jessie inside me doesn't want to loose you as a friend. No matter what happens, ever. Rachel, you've become my best friend. I like that we can talk, that we can go shopping, that we can just hang out together. I like the fact that you accept me for who I am. I've never met anyone like you and you really are special to me."

Jessie dropped her head and tried to wipe her tears with palms of her hands. Rachel leaned back and pulled several tissues from a box on the table. She handed them to Jessie.

"Thanks," she mumbled softly as she wiped her eyes. "God I probably look like a wreck."

"No," Rachel replied gently, "you're beautiful. But you have to go Jess, I need to apologize to your brother, okay?"

"Okay," Jessie replied as she stood up from the couch. "Bye," she whispered.

Jessie walked slowly back to her apartment. Once inside she pulled her wig off and set her heels inside the bedroom door. She padded softly back to her bathroom to remove her makeup.

As she looked in the mirror she looked at the bags under her eyes. For the first time in over a year the heartache was back. She wondered if he could stand the pain again. Was she falling in love with this woman? She couldn't get her out of her mind. And now this, she felt like she was all twisted up inside.

Jessie, now Jason, splashed cold water into his eyes then he grabbed a towel and dried his face. He knew that no matter what, Rachel had become a big part of his life. He would have to wait and see how much she was willing to let him be a part of hers.

He heard a soft knock on his front door. He walked out of the bathroom and through his living room. As the door opened he saw Rachel smiling meekly, standing in the hallway.

"Can I come in?" she asked softly.

"Of course," he replied and stood back so that she could walk into his living room.

She walked over to the couch and sat down, tucking her bare feet beneath her.

"Jason, I need to apologize," she started but stopped when Jason reached across and set a finger on her lips.

"I know. I was just so worried," he replied. "I thought I said something that made you angry or did something to piss you off. I didn't know. And then I began to fear that you might be hurt, like somebody messed you up again and I was almost sick with worry," he explained. "Then when I saw you hide your face and run off yesterday…"

"Jason, I am so sorry," she interrupted.

"Rachel, I care about you, I really do. If I make you angry or I hurt you, I need to know, okay? Please don't ever shut me out like that again. I just can't bare it."

Rachel reached across and wrapped her arms around his neck. She pulled him into a tight embrace and held him close.

"Jessie told me that I was her best friend tonight," she murmured into his ear. "I want you to know that you have become my best friend. I have never felt like this with anyone before I met you, not ever. From the moment I saw you stand in my heels and walk to your terrace door I knew that I had met someone who was going to change my life forever, and you have. Thank you."

They stayed like that, just holding one another, for a long time. Until finally Jason's stomach growled and Rachel giggled.

"Okay, I apologize for my rude stomach," he said with a grin. "Do you want to go out and get dinner?"

"Is it too late for that Indian restaurant?"

"Not if we hurry."

They quickly grabbed their coats and dashed out of the apartment building and headed for Jason's car. They walked through the restaurant and once again the exotic aromas of Indian cuisine assailed their senses.

"Mmm, I can't wait," she moaned as she slipped into the booth and picked up her menu.

"The last time we were here was nearly a month ago."

"Yes, our first date," she murmured looking up from the menu. "Kismet, I believe you called it."

"It still is," he replied and they both blushed.

"What are you getting?"

"I'm open for suggestions," he replied.

"How about we get the set dinner for two like we did last time," she said with a bright smile.

"Perfect." He motioned the waiter to join them.

After the waiter left Rachel reached across and took Jason's hands in hers. "So tell me about Karen Rolands."

He looked at Rachel and paused a moment as if collecting his thoughts. He smiled at her wistfully then began to tell his story.

"One night my parents put 'the ultimatum', as they called it, in front of me. It was either enlist or get out. So I got out. I packed a bag that night and walked out the door."

He took a sip of water. "You know, the funny thing is, I expected my mom to at least say something, to protest at least a little, but nothing, nada, not a peep. She just stood there with my father, watching me walk out the door, like I was some sort of distant relative who had overstayed his welcome. I must have walked a couple of miles that night trying to figure out what I was going to do. I was eighteen years old, fresh out of high school and legally considered an adult. But I had no idea what I was going to do next, no idea where my next step would take me."

Rachel gently squeezed his hands in hers. The smile on her face encouraged him to continue.

"It must have been about two in the morning when I finally worked my way around to understanding the depth of shit my stubbornness had gotten me into. I knew I had a full scholarship waiting for me at Case Western but that wasn't until the fall. I had three months to kill until then. I didn't think I wanted to spend it all sitting on a park bench in the middle of Dayton."

"I pulled out my cellphone to see what time it was and noticed that I had a couple of text messages. One was from a high school friend who wanted me to join him at another friend's house for a party and the other was from Karen Blanchard. Blanchard was her maiden name. Apparently Karen overheard her father talking to my mother about what had happened. She asked me in her text message what I was going to do? Well now it was two o'clock in the morning. I figured that she probably wouldn't be up but I thought, what the hell, and I sent her a text message anyway."

"Much to my surprise she called me back almost immediately. She wanted to know where I was and what I was doing. I played the macho role and puffed myself up. 'I don't care what the hell they say I'm going to blah, blah, blah. I think if she could have, she would have reached through the phone and slapped me right then and there," he added with a chuckle.

"My cousin and I used to play together when we were younger. Karen was a bit of a tomboy, a couple of years older than me, and a decade or so wiser. She acted more like my older sister than my cousin. We both went to high school together although she was a senior when I was a freshman. We'd hang out together from time to time when she wasn't out with her boyfriend or some of her girlfriends. At the time I thought she was pretty cool, even if she was a girl and could beat me in most sports."

"You know, I think my time in high school was the longest my parents ever spent in any one spot the entire time they were married. I finally had a chance to make a few friends and get to know my family."

"Anyway, Karen and I talked for over an hour before she suggested that I ask Grandma Kate if I could stay with her. Grandma Kate was my mom's mom. She was Karen's grandmother too because Karen's dad was my mom's older brother. Is this still making sense? I know that things can get confusing when you get into extended families."

"No, I'm fine."

About then the waiter returned with their dinner and Jason waited until they finished most of their meal to continue his story.

"So I waited until around seven that morning to call Grandma Kate. But by that time Karen had already called her and filled her in on all the details, at least as much as she knew anyway. So I spent my summer with Grandma Kate and that fall I went off to college. My folks moved out of Ohio shortly after I left home. My dad was issued orders to go to Germany and my Mom ended up at Fort Dix."

"Wow, so how did you end up in Cleveland?"

"I followed a girl there I met in school. I thought at the time that she was the love of my life.

She had a job offer from an accounting firm that did a lot of government contracts so it looked like a sweet deal. As I look back on it now, all she really wanted from me was for me to fix things and play 'the house bunny' while she was shacking up with the acquisitions manager at her work. I was her lackey she kept dangling carrots in front of to keep me preoccupied while she got herself knocked up. It took me two years and a good hard slap in the face from Karen to realize what was happening. I guess you can imagine that I have big issues with trust."

Rachel smiled serenely with glistening eyes as Jason continued with his story.

"I love my cousin dearly," he said with a sigh. "She has such a wonderful, caring family. After my crash and burn they helped me pick up the pieces but the damage was done. I couldn't stay there anymore, I couldn't be anywhere near that girl. For the longest time I didn't talk to anyone, beyond the cursory hello and goodbye. I was finishing up my third year of teaching high school English and the only people I spoke to on regular basis were my students. I had to get out of there. Karen knew that, but she hated to see me go. So she came down the other day hoping that I would change my mind and move back."

"I know," Rachel said, her cheeks were damp. "I saw her through your kitchen window and made a complete fool of myself."

"No you didn't. Besides, I probably would have made the same mistake," he replied reaching out to take her hand. "I'm glad Jessie was able to set things right."

"Me too." She paused a moment then looked up at Jason. "So, what did you tell her? About moving back to Cleveland I mean?"

"I told her I've met someone," he said gazing into her glistening eyes. "I told her that I didn't know where it's was going to go yet but I wanted to give it some time."

"Yeah, me too," she added with a growing smile.

"She said she wants to meet you sometime," he added picking up his water glass and taking another sip.

"Well we're not going to Cleveland," she replied quickly and emphatically, "I hear the weather is bad up there for people like us."

Jason choked back a laugh as he almost spit water across the table. He nodded his head and grinned at her sheepishly. "I agree!" He wiped his mouth with a cloth.

"Maybe she can meet us half way, like Louisville or someplace…for coffee or something," she added with a mischievous grin.

"I like that. I like that very much, and I think she might like that idea too."

When they returned from the restaurant they climbed the three flights of stairs hand in hand once again.

"Do you want to finish the evening on the terrace sharing a bottle of cheap wine?" she asked with a grin.

"Yes, I do, very much."

As Rachel opened her apartment door she looked across at Jason and smiled. "See you in a minute on the terrace?"

A minute later they both walked out their terrace doors. He stepped over the low fence, opened the wine, and joined her at her table.

"We're celebrating my latest promotion at work," she said with a broad grin.

"Congratulations. Does it come with a corner office?"

"Not yet, but I'm moving in that direction. At least I'm not in the basement anymore." She laughed and poured the wine.

Jason paused a moment and studied Rachel's face then his lips formed a wry smile.

"What?" She was aware that he had been staring at her.

"I'm curious," he said softly, "and you don't have to answer if you are uncomfortable, or you think I'm prying, or whatever." He paused a moment and looked into her eyes. He figured that she knew this question would eventually come up. What he didn't know was how she might react. "What's it like to be who you are?"

She smiled wistfully, let out a low whistle, and settled back into her chair. She paused a moment to gather her thoughts, looking out at the evening sky. "Some days, like tonight, on this terrace sharing a bottle of wine with my best friend, it's rather wonderful," she replied smiling. "Other days it's really horrible."

He sat up and looked at her glistening eyes. "Shit, I'm sorry. I didn't want to spoil the evening. Let's talk about something else."

"It's fine. You haven't spoiled a thing," she replied sweetly. "You've been perfect." Rachel turned in her chair and reached out to take Jason's hand. "There's a lot of confusion and fear out in the world about people like me. Sometimes it ends in bruises on the outside and sometimes there are scars on the inside where no one can see them. The scars are the ones that take the longest to heal."

Rachel gazed softly into Jason's eyes. "You once told me that you have issues with trust, and so do I. I've been devastated more times than I want to remember. My sister Hanna calls me an incurable romantic and I suppose she's right. I guess that's why I jumped to conclusions when I saw you with your cousin."

She paused a moment and looked into his eyes. "Jason I still can't believe that this, you and I as friends, is real. Good things like this don't happen to me, not like this. I'm just waiting for the other shoe to drop."

"Nah, it's not going to happen," he said with conviction, "because we won't let it happen. We're not going to force anything. Let's take it slow and easy."

"Enjoy the moment and not worry about tomorrow?"

"Exactly," he agreed. "Oh, and speaking of shoes…"

"I was just going to ask you to ask Jessie if she wanted to go shopping with me? We leave for the Bahamas next Thursday and I haven't a thing to wear," she said striking a pose with her hand across her forehead dramatically.

"Of course, when?"

"Tomorrow after work," she replied with a twinkle in her eyes. "I need a new swimming suit and a sundress for midnight walks on the beach too."

"No shoes?"

"Of course I need a pair of new shoes! I think some fading Hollywood actress once said, 'Dawling, you can never have enough shoes,' and I believe she's right."

=EIGHT=

Jason raced home after his last class on Thursday and bounded up the three flights of stairs two steps at a time. He raced into his bathroom and jumped into the shower.

A few minutes later he stood in front of the mirror shaving as close as he could. He was fortunate enough to have fair hair so the process wasn't all that arduous but still stubble was annoying when you tried to apply a smooth foundation.

He dashed into the bedroom and pulled open his closet door. A moment later he stood looking into a full-length mirror wearing a loose cashmere sweater over a nice pair of fitted slacks.

"Hmm, very nice," he heard Rachel say as she peeked around the bedroom door. "I like that sweater, casual but very smart, in a gender neutral sort of way. Nicely done."

"Thank you," he replied with a smirk. "I said no dresses and I meant it."

"Just the shoes, I know," she replied. "Are you

ready?"

"Just the makeup, can you help make the magic happen?"

She smiled serenely and nodded towards the living room. "My dressing table is all yours Jessie."

"Wait, I need some hose and my shoes," he said as lifted his wig off the wig stand on his dresser and took her hand.

"We'll come back for them. Come on, Sarah closes her place early on nights like this."

He reluctantly followed her out of his apartment and into hers glancing around the hallway to make sure that no one could see him.

Twenty minutes later Rachel was applying the finishing touches and the transformation was complete.

"There, as beautiful as ever," she said with a coy smile adjusting Jessie's wig and pulling out a few curls.

"Thank you Rachel, you are truly a magician," she said looking at her reflection in the mirror.

Rachel leaned forward and kissed Jessie on the cheek. "Now come on, don't dawdle, we need to get going if we want to have time to shop."

"I'll meet you outside in a couple of minutes, I have to put on some shoes," she said rushing out of her front door.

Three minutes later she met her in the hallway as she closed the front door. She had on a pair of knee-high hose under her slacks and a pair of ballet flats. They were the same ones she borrowed from Rachel two weeks ago when they first went shoe shopping. She glanced down at his shoes and smirked.

"You want me to wreck in heels?"

"I didn't say a word," she replied as her smirk

grew into a broad grin.

"I thought we were in a hurry," she said pushing Rachel to lead the way down the stairs. She giggled all the way down the first flight.

They arrived at the Shoe Boutique shortly before five, which according to Rachel would give them just over an hour to find the perfect pair of sandals for the beach.

Jessie made a beeline for the heels and started trying on a pair of five-inch 'Rachel Roy's'. They screamed for the chance to caress her feet. She slipped them on and admired the look in the mirror while Rachel shook her head with a wry grin and walked away.

Thirty minutes later, shoeboxes in hand, Rachel found Jessie at the back of the store trying on a pair of pumps from the clearance rack. The stiletto heels were at least five and a half inches tall.

"You really go for the tall ones don't you?"

Jessie walked in front of the mirror admiring the way the shoes looked. "They make my feet look small," she whispered with a shrug. "And they are totally sexy."

"How much are they?"

"Only fifty nine dollars, I paid attention this time," she replied with a twinkle in her eyes.

"That sounds like a bargain." She paused a moment and looked around to see if anyone was nearby. "Jessie, are you going with Jason and me to the Bahamas? Because if you are, you should look for some sandals."

Jessie stopped and glanced over her shoulder at Rachel. She turned and gave her a gentle hug. Then he leaned back and smiled sweetly.

"Thank you for asking but no, that's just for you two, I'd just be a third wheel," she replied earnestly. "We'll go to someplace special just the two of us when you get back, okay?"

"Okay," Rachel replied her smile broadened and she gave Jessie another hug.

"But I do want details, lots of details," Jessie added with a wicked grin and a whisper.

Rachel smiled winsomely and shrugged her shoulders, her eyes twinkling with mischief. "Bring your shoes up front I want you to meet Sarah," she said picking up Jessie's flats and putting them in a shoebox.

Jessie followed Rachel to the front of the store sashaying up the aisle in her stiletto heels. Behind the cash register was a buxom young woman with bright red hair and half a dozen piercings on each of her ears. She had tattoos running from the wrist up both of her arms and an assortment of rings on each hand.

"Jessie," Rachel said gesturing to the girl behind the counter, "this is Sarah. Sarah, this is Jessie, a very good friend of mine who continues to keep me out of trouble and is in love with your store."

Jessie blushed bright crimson and reached forward to shake Sarah's hand. "Hi."

"Hi back at you," Sarah replied "You're going to like those Rachel Roy's and the Sergio Rossi's look good on you."

"Thanks," Jessie murmured with a coy smile.

"I think she'll take both," Rachel said as she set her boxes on the counter alongside of Jessie's.

"Is this your first time in here?" Sarah asked Jessie.

"No, I was in here a few weeks back and bought a pair of red pumps," she replied softly trying to keep her voice as feminine as she could.

"Good, I love to see a repeat customer," Sarah added with a grin.

"Oh, she's a repeat customer all right," Rachel chided. "If I don't keep an eye on her she'll buy out the whole store," she added laughing.

Jessie merely rolled her eyes as Sarah finished ringing up their purchase. Jessie handed her credit card over to Sarah and whispered, "my treat," to Rachel with a wink.

Rachel started to protest but then she smiled demurely and whispered, "thank you."

Jessie wore the stilettos out of the store and strutted across the parking lot to the car.

"You are shameless in those heels," Rachel said playfully rubbing Jessie's shoulder.

"Yes I am but I simply adore them. I'd wear them all the time except for the damn social construct that seems to prevent it."

"So, do you wear them around the apartment?"

She turned and leaned against the car door. "Actually, no I don't. I only like to wear them when we're together. I know that sounds weird but somehow I think wearing them all the time would take away the magic."

Jessie reached into one of the bags full of boxes and pulled out the flats she borrowed from Rachel the first time they went shoe shopping. "I really ought to buy my own pair of flats," she said slipping off the stilettos and placing them in a box.

"Just keep them. It will give me an excuse to borrow those Rachel Roy's," Rachel added with a devilish grin, "they scream trouble."

She grabbed Jessie's arm and pulled her around the car. "Come on, let's go to the mall." She walked around to sit in the passenger seat. "I still have that dress to find."

"And a skimpy bikini," Jessie added with a grin.

After they ran in and out of several of smaller boutique shops they stopped in Forever 21 and found a delightful sun wrap that fit Rachel remarkably well.

While she tried on several other dresses Jessie wandered over to the swimwear section and gathered several bikinis for Rachel to try on. She walked back over to the fitting rooms and waited for her to come out.

A moment later Rachel appeared wearing a lovely blue dress that gathered asymmetrically. It accented her breasts and the curve of her hips nicely.

"Now that one is a keeper," Jessie said enthusiastically and handed Rachel her bikini selection. "Here try these on."

She blushed crimson and took the swimwear towards the fitting room. She turned at the fitting room door and looked back at Jessie.

"I'm not going to show them to you out here," she said firmly. "So you'll just have to accept whichever one I choose."

"No problem, I'm sure that they all will look stunning on you."

A few minutes later Rachel walked out of the fitting room with several dresses and one of the bikinis wrapped up hidden in the bundle.

"Which one did you choose?"

"You'll just have to wait until we get to the

beach."

The next stop was Victoria's Secret. After a thorough search through the bras and panties Rachel grabbed Jessie's hand and pulled her towards the dressing room.

"What are you doing?" she asked looking a bit alarmed.

"I thought you'd like to help me," Rachel said with a wicked grin.

"You are such a tease. Now hurry up, I'm getting hungry. I'll be over there checking out the lingerie."

Rachel put on a mock pout and then she smiled demurely at Jessie. Jessie shook her head and smirked. "You are still such a tease," she repeated with a grin.

She laughed and ducked into the changing room.

After she spent way too much money in Victoria's Secret, Jessie drove her over to a little Italian restaurant for dinner. "I've been wanting to go to this place since I first spotted it when I moved here," she said browsing through the menu. "A colleague at work told me its one of the best in town."

A few minutes later the waiter left with their order returning moments later with a bottle of nice Chianti. He poured the wine then disappeared behind a screen to welcome new customers.

Two men walked across the dining room towards a table that apparently had been reserved for them by the windows.

"Shit," Rachel whispered ducking her face behind the wine menu. "Those guys over there are from my work."

"Really?"

"Quick, trade places with me after I take a trip to the restroom," she pleaded and Jessie nodded.

As she stood up Jessie stood as well. She moved to the other side of the table as Rachel left for the restroom. Several moments later Rachel returned and managed to slide into her seat unnoticed.

"They didn't even look up," Jessie said leaning forward to whisper.

"Good," Rachel muttered, looking tense.

The waiter returned again with their salad and the main course shortly afterwards. They quickly finished their dinner and were about to leave when the men from Rachel's office decided to stop by their table.

"Good evening, ladies," the taller of the two said as his friend joined him. He was holding a glass of wine and the remainder of another bottle of Chianti. "Rob and I wanted to know if you girls would like some company? You two looked so lonely over here."

Jessie looked across the table and shook her head slightly. Was this how guys try to pick up girls? No wonder men usually strike out.

"Hi, my name's Bill," said the taller man as he extended his hand to Rachel. He sat their bottle on the table.

"And I'm Rob," said the other man reaching over to shake Jessie's hand. Jessie was beginning to panic as the men pulled chairs over to join them. She looked a bit frightened as she glanced across at Rachel.

Rachel wasn't faring much better; these guys were, after all, from her company. Thankfully it didn't look like either one of them recognized her.

She replied with a simple, "Hi, I'm Rachel and this is Jessie," she said gesturing towards Jessie with a modest smile.

Jessie managed a pleasant smile and nod but she didn't offer much more for fear that her voice would give her away.

"How about we buy you girls another bottle of wine? This Chianti is really quite good," Rob said with a grin.

Jessie watched Bill's eyes rove over Rachel in a way that suggested he had more on his mind than pleasant conversation and another bottle of red wine.

Rachel smiled demurely. "Thank you Rob, you're very sweet, but no thanks. I'm in a committed relationship with someone right now and I don't want you to get the wrong idea."

Bill looked a bit disappointed but then he joined Rob and both men smiled at Jessie.

"The someone I'm in a relationship with is her." Rachel gestured towards Jessie and blushed slightly.

"Oh, I see," muttered Rob looking disappointed. "Well, you girls enjoy your dinner."

"Yeah," Bill added, retrieving the bottle of wine. "If you change your mind we'll be at the bar." Both men stood up and replaced the chairs they brought over from another table then they sauntered off in the direction of the restaurant bar.

Jessie drew in a big breath and let it out slowly. "I don't think I've ever been so frightened in all my life," she said blushing bright crimson. "I felt like Rob was undressing me the whole time he sat there."

"From the look in his eyes, I think he was," Rachel replied with a giggle. "Do you want me to call them back?"

"God no, that's not even funny!" Jessie hissed, her eyes flared with embarrassment.

"Oh come on," Rachel chided, "you have to admit it was a huge compliment, Rob looked like he was really interested."

"He was only interested in the illusion you've created, my dear," she replied with a smirk. "I'm sure Rob would have been disappointed to discover what the total package contained."

"Most likely Bill would have reacted the same way," Rachel added. "That's why dating boys can be such a pain. They all have some sort of ideal of who and what a woman is. When they find that I don't match that ideal they get angry, sometimes violent."

"What about women? Do women react the same way?"

"No, most women don't make a scene but I immediately feel a 'push-back' when they realize who or what I am. At best it's disappointing," she murmured softly. "When I really have an attraction to someone, or think that something could develop between us, it's the worst. I crawl back into my shell and hide out with a bucket of chocolate ice cream for a couple of days."

"Do you really do that?" Jessie looked incredulous. "I thought that was a Hollywood myth."

"Well, myth or not, it's what I do."

"Does it help?"

"A little, but mostly it deadens the pain. And then I have to work off the pounds I gained in they gym over the next four weeks."

"Rachel, you're a mess."

"I am a mess," she replied. "And right now I'm a happy mess, so I don't care."

Jessie motioned for the waiter to bring the check. A few minutes later they walked by the bar on their way out of the restaurant. Near the far end of the bar they saw Bill and his friend Rob chatting up a couple of college co-eds dressed like they were on the prowl for a pair of lawyers.

"Looks like the boys are going to get lucky tonight," Jessie said with a smirk.

"I wonder if the girls will too?"

Jessie started the car then reached up and pulled off his clip-on earrings with an "Ouch". She sat there rubbing her ears as the motor warmed up.

"You really do need to get your ears pierced Jess," Rachel said with a snicker. Jessie rolled her eyes.

The following morning Rachel sat in her I.T. office dressed as Ray. Outside in the corridor she overheard two of the junior members of the law firm talking in the hallway.

"Last night was a total bust," said the first voice that Rachel recognized as Bill.

"Totally, those girls in the bar were just looking for somebody to pick up the tab," said the other voice who sounded like Rob.

"It's too bad those two we saw in the restaurant were lezzies," said Bill. "Rachel looked totally hot. I would have enjoyed going down on that."

My god, do you ever listen to yourself? Rachel sat there shaking her head. Those two clowns didn't even try to make their conversation private.

"I just wanted into Jessie's panties," Rob ruminated. "I wonder if she was wearing a thong."

"You and thongs, man, you're twisted," Bill

replied as he slapped Rob on the back.

"Hey, I just think they make their butts look sexy," Rob said as both men walked off down the corridor away from Rachel's office. "No panty line you know…" His voice faded as they walked away.

Rachel wondered if she should share this with Jason? The thought brought with it an impish smile. She decided she'd wait until she saw Jessie again.

The phone rang and she was pulled back into the real world of 'fixing their little boo-boos'.

At home, over the rest of the week, Rachel and Jason fell into a regular routine, alternating back and forth between who cooked and who washed the dishes. Most of their evenings were spent in front of the television although recently Jason started writing again.

"What are you working on?" She leaned over his laptop as she finished drying the last of the dishes.

Jason sat on a stool at the island counter with his laptop propped up on a small stand. "A fantasy young audience story."

"What's it about?"

"It's a high adventure, sword and sorcery tale about a young girl who lost her parents in a car crash and ends up living with her aunt in Arizona," he said looking up at her from across the counter. "She's your typical inquisitive teenager who finds out that her aunt collects these curious magical antiques and keeps them hidden away in her attic. She ends up on this journey to a far off land in search of a powerful crystal to save an ancient village from evil."

"What's it called?"

"Right now it's called Amanda."

"That's it? Not much of a title."

"I haven't finished it yet," he said nonchalantly. "The book usually tells me what it wants to be called while I'm creating it. It just hasn't spoken to me yet."

"You're just a little crazy aren't you?"

"A little but that's what's so appealing about my character," he added with a smirk.

"Yeah, character, that's a good description for you." She turned back to the sink and wiped the last bowl.

"I never did ask you, do you have a hobby or a passion?"

"I do actually but I haven't paid much attention to it for years." She put the plates back into the cupboard.

"Perhaps you should. What is it?"

"I like to make fused glass jewelry." She turned around and leaned on the counter next to him.

"Wow, really?"

"Yeah, when I was in college I took a couple of art classes to clear my head from all the computer code I'd been cramming in there. When I was a kid my uncle was a glass artist. He used to have a kiln in his garage that he fused glass in every so often. He let me play one year and I was totally hooked. So I took a couple of art classes when I got to college. One of them was a glass blowing class. That was totally awesome. We learned how to gather the glass on pipes and open up the molten glass into a bottle form. Then we'd transfer the glass from one pipe to another. It was so cool. Wait," she said jumping up, "I'll show you a couple of pieces I did."

She ran back to her apartment and a couple of minutes later the terrace door slid open and she walked back into his living room with a bowl and a vase.

"They're kind of heavy and clunky because I only took the class for one semester but it was a total blast, pun intended."

"These are really nice," he said holding the vase and admiring the pattern in the glass. "I love the pattern, how did you do that?"

"There's trick to it, of course. You set ground glass in a pattern on the forming table and roll the hot glass into it before you begin to blow the form. As it expands it melts the ground colored glass and begins to make the pattern. It's very irregular, each bottle is unique when you don't use a mold."

"Beautiful."

"Thank you," she said taking the vase and setting it on the counter.

"But I thought you said you liked fusing glass?"

"That was the other class, we took sheets of fusible glass and layered them up in bits and pieces. Then we put them in a kiln and fired them until they melted and fused together. Here," she said pointing to a pin she wore on her jacket and a necklace around her neck. "Both of these are fused pieces that I made."

"Earrings too?"

"Uh-huh, earrings too," she replied.

"It almost makes me want to get my ears pierced," he said with a grin. "Almost."

"Get them pierced and I'll make something especially for you," she responded with a tempting smile.

"Hmmm."

=NINE=

Thursday finally arrived for Rachel's first big adventure. They sat in the plane as it taxied to the end of the runway. It was her first time in a plane and the first time she'd ever been out of the country.

Rachel looked at Jason with a 'deer in the headlights' sort of look. She was experiencing the classic 'white-knuckle-flight' syndrome and he tried hard not to show how amused he was for fear that she would just punch him. She might be a girl but she could throw a mean punch.

"Thank you for doing this but at the same time if something happens I'll never forgive you," she muttered through clenched teeth.

He held her hands and smiled sympathetically. "It'll be all right," he said trying to reassure her.

"Right," she said still looking tense.

"You're safer here than driving a car."

"You can't drive a car to the Bahamas."

The engines throttled up and the plane began to vibrate as it started to roll down the runway. Rachel's eyes were squeezed shut; it was nerve-wracking and exhilarating all at the same time. A moment later the plane lifted off the ground and the landing gear locked away with a loud thump. "Open your eyes," he said over the roar of the engines. "You're missing everything!"

She held her hands over her face and then she peeked out between her fingers at the ground as it rapidly receded from the plane. Suddenly all her fears were gone and she was glued to the window, taking snapshot after snapshot with her pocket camera. Rachel turned to Jason with a gleam in her eyes. "That is fantastic!" she shouted with glee.

"I told you didn't I?"

"We're flying! We're going so high," she said excitedly.

"We'll be much higher before we get there," he said nonchalantly.

"How much higher?"

"Probably around thirty thousand feet, that's usually where they fly commercial flights."

"Thirty thousand?"

"That way if we loose a wing we have longer to figure out what to do before we hit the water," he said teasing her.

She smacked him on the arm.

"That was not even funny, Jason," she retorted smacking him again.

Several hours later the plane began its descent through the light puffy clouds that hovered over Nassau. Rachel gripped Jason's arm with a near death grip.

She started to squeeze her eyes tightly shut but Jason shouted at her.

"You'll miss it if you keep your eyes shut," he chided her with a grin.

She gathered her courage and looked out the window. It was frightening and exhilarating all at the same time. The plane touched down with a little bounce and then the brakes slowed it down.

Eventually the plane moved onto the taxiway and rolled to a stop at their gate.

"I want to learn how to fly!" shouted Rachel as she left the boarding area in the Nassau airport.

"What?"

"I do Jason! I want to learn how to fly! That was magnificent!" she shouted with glee.

"My god, I've unleashed a monster," Jason chuckled.

"I really do! Let's find a place where I can learn to fly when we get back home," she repeated as she hugged his arm and kissed his cheek. "We'll both take lessons, okay?"

"Okay, okay, we'll look into it as soon as we get back," he said laughing at her enthusiasm, "I promise."

Rachel nearly skipped down the walkway towards baggage claim.

A cab ride and a short hike brought them to their hotel. The check in went on without a hitch. They climbed the three flights of stairs to their rooms with a familiar grin on their faces.

A moment later both Rachel and Jason stood at the door of their room that led to a terrace overlooking the ocean several blocks away. A low block wall just like the one at home separated the terrace between the two adjoining rooms. Jason looked across at Rachel with a huge grin on his face and Rachel turned to him with a smile that seemed to hang off her ears.

"It's just like home!" they exclaimed in unison then laughed.

"Come on, let's check out the local cuisine, I'm famished." She slipped on a pair of flip-flops and turned towards her door.

"I talked to the clerk at the desk and she recommended a place just a block away. Their specialty is conch."

"Everybody's specialty is conch down here but let's try it anyway," he said locking his room.

After dinner they took a cab over to the tourist strip on Paradise Island. They went club hoping for most of the night finishing up at a hotel pool bar where you could swim and drink until you were drunk or drowned, whichever came first.

They ended the evening standing, well more like swaying from the alcohol, in the hallway at the doors to their rooms. Jason was smiling like a drunken sailor and Rachel giggled like a schoolgirl.

He leaned over to give her a goodnight kiss and nearly fell on his face.

"I think we should just leave it like this, sweetie," she said watching him stand up slowly trying to stead himself against the wall.

"You're probably right," he slurred. "Damn I'm plastered. This is probably why I don't drink," he gushed as he leaned back towards the door to his room.

"G'Night beautiful," he slurred more than said as he fumbled with his room key.

Rachel continued to giggle as she watched Jason try to figure out which end was up on his room key.

Once inside Jason flopped down on the bed and passed out. He didn't move a muscle until nature demanded that he get up to pee around three in the morning, and even then he tripped several times walking, or actually stumbling from the toilet back to his bed.

The next day the sun streamed through the terrace door and woke him up earlier than he wanted. He stumbled out onto the terrace and rubbed the sleep out of his eyes. It felt like his head was nearly the size of the doorway he just walked through. He walked slowly back into his room and picked up the phone to call room service.

A few minutes later a tray was delivered with a much-needed carafe of coffee, some toast, and the morning paper.

Jason tapped on the connecting door that led from his room to hers. "Breakfast on the terrace," he said softly, "if you're up."

He placed the tray on the table on the terrace and poured a cup of coffee when he heard Rachel's terrace door slide open.

He held up the carafe. "Coffee?"

"God yes, my head is much larger than it should be at this hour of the morning," she mumbled as she stepped over the dividing wall and slumped down in the chair near the table.

"Remind me not to drink like that again," he said rubbing his forehead.

"Remind me not to drink like that too," she replied rubbing her forehead as well. "But it was fun," she added with a sheepish grin.

"Yeah it was."

Later that morning, they decided to check out

the local shopping district. Jason laughed as he held up a bundle of t-shirts. "I've heard of the gold standard to support an economy, I think the Bahamas is on the t-shirt standard. I've never seen so many t-shirts in my whole life!"

"Look at this." She held up a little statue shaped like a monkey and made out of coconut shells. "This is insane."

"I love the fact that they sell snow globes in the Bahamas."

They bought a few t-shirts and a couple of other typical tourist items then Rachel suggested they head over to Paradise Island and see what kinds of shops were available over there.

She pulled him into several dress shops before they landed in a shoe shop.

"You are so mean," Jason grumbled, "pulling me in here instead of Jessie." He was almost pouting.

"Jessie said she didn't want to be a third wheel, but that doesn't mean I can't find the perfect sandal without her."

"I suppose, as long as I get to borrow them when we get back."

She smiled an enigmatic smile and gave him an air kiss then turned her attention to the array of sandals on display.

He shrugged and bit his lip then he wandered off to look at the selection of flip-flops.

The next shop over was a costume jewelry store with a huge selection of earrings. She pulled him over to the sales counter and pointed to the sign that said 'free ear piercing with a pair of earrings'.

"You said you'd get them done, why not now?"

He stood there a moment and looked at her with

a grimace then as if finally coming to a decision, he shrugged his shoulders. "Okay, but on one condition."

"What's that?"

"You have to wear that bikini I bought for you in Northport on the beach today." He couldn't help but grin mischievously.

"Agreed as long as I get to pick the beach."

"Deal."

While he was sitting in the chair getting his ears jabbed with a sharp needle Rachel bought a pair of simple crystal stud earrings for him as a starter.

"These are cute and they'll look good on you," she said holding them close to his ears. "Remember to keep the piercings clean and you have to keep the posts in your ears until they heal."

That afternoon they talked to one of the hotel concierges. Rachel was hoping to find a secluded beach away from the crowds. The concierge nodded, called a cab driver up from the queue, and asked him to take them to a coral beach. It was on the far side of the island and almost private.

Rachel smiled and thanked the concierge then she climbed into the back seat of the cab beside Jason.

Twenty-five minutes later they were both standing on a small rock outcropping near a narrow strip of sand that wove its way around that part of the island. The sun was bright and the breezes light. It was nearly perfect.

Jason grabbed the bag full of snorkel gear, towels, and clothing from the cab. He picked his way through the rocks towards the beach while Rachel paid the cab driver. She tipped him well enough to encourage him to come back for them in a couple of hours. She waved goodbye to the taxi and turned to follow Jason onto the sand. "Where are we going to change clothes?" She looked around. There didn't seem to be anything in the way of an obvious shelter.

"Over there," he pointed towards a stand of palm trees and some bushes. "See if that place will work."

Rachel grabbed the clothing bag and walked briskly across the sand towards the tiny shelter. A moment or two later she emerged wearing her bikini.

Jason stood totally in awe of her in the suit she chose. It was skimpy and seductive all at the same time. It hid little and enhanced a lot. His pants were getting very tight as he watched her walk towards him across the sand. He glanced down at her crotch and wondered how she kept it hidden but he decided not to ask. She blushed enough without having to answer something like that.

"Wow, you look fabulous," he said blushing at his schoolboy bluster. "You have no reason to be shy on any beach sweetie, you are gorgeous and that suit is stunning.

"Thank you," she said blushing bright crimson. "But if it's all the same to you, I still like my privacy."

He had laid out several towels and pulled the bag with their snorkeling gear over to anchor the towels. He opened a sand umbrella they bought earlier in the day and he pitched it to give them a little seclusion from the road. She sat down beneath the umbrella and waited until Jason changed into his swimming trunks. A moment later Jason flopped down next to her under the umbrella.

"So, have you ever been snorkeling before?" He

sorted through the gear in the bag.

"Nope, I'm a newbie."

Jason glanced down at her perfectly formed breasts and blushed when he glanced up to see her watching him. He grabbed a spare towel and laid it over his crotch.

"I'm sorry, I don't mean to be rude but that swim suit is just…well, it's totally doing a number on my libido," he stammered blushing a deeper shade of crimson.

It was her turn to blush as she leaned forward and kissed him tenderly on the cheek. "Thank you Jason, that's very sweet."

Taking in a big breath and blowing it out quickly he set about removing all the packaging from their swim fins, masks, and snorkels.

"It's a good thing we bought these before we left," he said tugging at a label, "the prices down here are astronomical. Here, take this mask and fit it to your face then adjust the straps until it's held snugly against you face but not too tight."

"When we get in the water I want you to spit in the mask and rub it all around the inside then rinse it out with sea water."

"Why?"

"So that it doesn't fog up when you're underwater." "Here," he said handing her the snorkel tube. "Slip this through that rubber loop. It will hold the tube in position when you're floating on the surface."

Her eyes sparkled with excitement as she watched him set up the equipment.

"You do know how to swim don't you?"

"Of course," she replied. "I always wanted to be

a life guard when I was in high school but, well…it just didn't work out. I took the courses privately anyway."

"Great, that will all come in handy now. If this works out well maybe we an go scuba diving tomorrow."

"I've always wanted to try that!"

He managed to subdue his baser desires while he concentrated on finishing the adjustments to their gear. Finally, with masks, snorkels, and fins, they duck-walked down to the water's edge and waddled out into the surf.

A minute later they were in water that was deep enough to swim and they were off heading for their first aquatic adventure, a coral head just fifty yards away in crystal clear water. "It's like swimming in a fish tank," she exclaimed as she came up for air.

"Yeah, isn't it marvelous!"

They spent the afternoon bobbing around several coral heads looking at fish and searching for seashells until they were exhausted. Eventually they walked hand in hand back to the road and waited for Richard their cab driver to take them back to their hotel.

=TEN=

After dinner they strolled on the beach walking barefoot in the surf. Jason pulled her round into his arms and kissed her passionately on the lips. They lingered like that for a moment longer then he leaned back to gaze into her beautiful eyes.

Her eyes were beginning to glisten. Tiny teardrops fell across her cheeks like pearls that twinkled in the moonlight.

"What's wrong Rachel? Did I do something wrong?"

"No, never. I'm just a little scared."

"Why? Of what?"

"Everything, you, me, us, this moment, it all makes me nervous Jason." She was noticeably shaking.

"Nothing has to happen that you don't want to happen Rachel. Remember, we said let's take it slow and easy. We're going to enjoy the moment and not worry about tomorrow, right?"

"But I'm afraid that if we go too slow you'll get

tired of me and want to run away."

"Oh Rachel." He shook his head with a sweet smile. "I'm not running anywhere, sweetheart." He held out his arms. "I'm standing right here. And I'm just as scared as you are. If you'll remember I haven't had much luck in the romance department either. I thought that girl in Cleveland was the one for me but she's nothing compared to how I feel about you."

"It's just that I've never been this physical with a man before, I don't know how to react."

"You're a virgin?" He tried to mask his concern.

"Yes. Every man I've ever been with has never wanted me to be this intimate. As soon as they learned about me, the real me, they run as fast as they can for the exit. I really care about you and I don't want to do something foolish to screw things up."

"I feel exactly the same way, I don't want to screw things up either." He wrapped his arms around her neck.

"But I'm different."

"Shush," he interrupted, leaning in to kiss her on the lips. "You are truly beautiful Rachel." He leaned back, smiling. "You're unique and incredible and amazing. I told you before, sweetheart, you're my best friend. You've changed my life."

"But what if we mess things up?" she asked her voice still trembling.

"Then we'll just let Jessie find a way to fix it," he added with a grin.

She smiled sheepishly as he wrapped her in his arms. She rested her head on his chest and sighed.

"I know that deep down inside, you and Jessie are the same but somehow having your 'sister' at home with me makes us closer. I can't explain it any other way. Does it bother you that I'm close to Jessie but in a different way?"

"Yes and no. It's kind of weird, and I'm jealous of Jessie sometimes. You talk to her about things I fear you could never say to me. I know it's actually me in heels and a wig but it's still Jessie for both of us, which is what makes it kind of weird I suppose."

"I can't help it, Jason. When you're Jessie I can just relax in a way I can't with you or anyone else. I know that's weird but it's a girl thing. We're just made that way. We share intimate things with one another more freely than men. I guess its like a protection mechanism hard wired into our brains. We offer men the ultimate sacrifice of submission, the moment you embrace us and enter our bodies, in either love or lust. We have to feel that it's right. So we talk it through. "

"Do you share everything?" He looked a bit worried.

"Sometimes."

"Whoa, that's a little bit overwhelming."

"I would only tell Jessie, sweetheart. No one else, not even my sister Hanna," she added sheepishly. "She would never understand me like Jessie does. This sounds nuts doesn't it? But I wouldn't have it any other way."

"Thank you, Rachel, and you know," he assured her, "I'm sure that Jessie would never say anything to anyone as well."

As a quarter-moon rose in an indigo sky, he embraced her and kissed her again gently on the lips then he nuzzled his head on her shoulder. He could smell the sweetness of her perfume; he could feel the softness of her hair on his face. It just felt so right to hold her, to caress her, to never let her go.

They walked back to their hotel and up the three flights of stairs to their rooms. As Jason neared his room door he turned and looked at Rachel. "Join me for a glass of wine on the terrace?"

"I wouldn't miss it," she said softly, "but I need to change first."

Jason opened his door and walked into his room. He slipped out of his clothes and pulled on a t-shirt and a clean pair of shorts. He grabbed a bottle of wine from the counter near the television and picked up two plastic cups. Then he stepped out onto the terrace and opened the bottle with a pop.

He smiled as he thought of the surf splashing around them when he kissed her just minutes ago. He remembered the feeling of her full breasts pressed against his chest, his rigid cock pressed against her thigh. And finally, he thought of her cock growing hard against his stomach as she kissed him back. It was weird, strange and mesmerizing all at the same time.

He wanted her so badly. He wanted to touch her, to caress her, to know what it was like to make love to her. He knew she was unique but that was what excited him, even if he didn't really know why. It didn't matter. He loved her and he hoped that she loved him.

He heard the lock to the inner suite door unlatch. He froze as he stood listening, too excited to turn and see what was happening. The inner door that connected the two rooms opened and Rachel stepped into his room. Taking a big breath, Jason turned slowly to see her moving gracefully towards him.

She wore a long diaphanous robe of sheer white

silk that closed at the waist with a pink satin sash. Beneath it she wore a white teddy in satin with garter straps that held sheer white hose reaching up to her thighs. Her shoes were the same white sandals that she first put on his feet so many months ago while he played possum and pretended to sleep on his terrace.

She glided across the floor and joined him. Her hair flowing in gentle curls to caress her face and grace her shoulders. She was breath-taking and Jason stood stunned as he watched her move towards him.

"Happy Birthday," she said shyly handing him a card. It was tied with a pink ribbon and it matched a bow she held in her hand. With an impish smile, she stuck the pink bow above her heart and smiled demurely.

"How did you know?"

"I snuck a peek at your driver's license a couple of weeks ago when you weren't looking."

Jason opened his card and read it out loud. "Happy Birthday to my best friend. I hope that we have a lifetime of them to come." He leaned towards her and kissed her on her cheek. "Thank you, that's very sweet."

A smaller card fell out of the envelope and fluttered to land at his feet. He picked up and turned it over, looking curiously at her.

"Go ahead…open it," she urged with a whisper.

He opened the smaller envelope and pulled out a small card. "Your birthday gift is…me," he read slowly out loud and then looked up at her in wonder.

Her eyes were glistening as she smiled at him sweetly. She held out her arms and beaconed him towards her.

"I love you Jason," she whispered softly. "I

wanted this night to be special and I couldn't think of a better gift than me."

"Oh my sweet Rachel," His voice quavered with emotion. "Thank you. I love you so much." She held him tightly for a moment then she let him go. He slipped from her arms and took her hands in his to draw her into his room and towards his bed.

As she stood by the bed she began to undress but he put his hands on hers to stop her.

"Let me," he whispered, "I would love to unwrap this birthday present," he added with a twinkle in his eyes.

She stood silently and watched him carefully unbutton the robe to let it fall about her feet. He knelt down and unbuckled the straps on her sandals. She stepped out of them and he pushed them aside. He stood up then he began to undo the straps of her teddy. It fell away from her to reveal her full breasts arching upwards with her nipples erect.

He peeled the teddy down to fall away from the curve of her hips and collapse on the floor at her feet. She stood with open arms watching him intently, her eyes sparkling with anticipation.

She nestled in the pillows as she got into his bed and turned to watch him undress.

He slowly lifted the t-shirt off his body and pulled his shorts over his hips to let them fall to the floor.

He stood there a moment in only his briefs, admiring her beauty as she lay before him like a goddess. Then he reached down and pulled his briefs off to let them puddle around his feet. Her eyes sparkled with delight as she saw his cock spring from the confines of his briefs.

His heart was racing as he knelt in the bed to lie beside her; his hands slowly caressed her breasts and face. She moaned a moment then leaned over to kiss his hand as it caressed her cheek. Then she reached across to offer him the same caress, moving her hands like the wings of a butterfly to tickle and touch his chest and face.

He propped himself up on an elbow and leaned forward to take her left nipple into his mouth. He sucked and gently nibbled it to stand erect while his other hand kneaded her right nipple, pulling and pinching it between his finger and thumb. She arched her back as he caressed her breasts and uttered a soft low moan of pleasure.

He continued to suckle at her nipple as his hand trailed down her body towards her cock. He rubbed the growing mound beneath her panties; her cock was stiffening under all this attention. He caressed her more and her cock, now rigid and throbbing, began to leak pre-cum from the tip to leave a damp spot on her panties. He sat up and slowly removed her panties. He looked down at her and smiled.

"You are so beautiful Rachel, my heart is racing so fast I think it's caught in my throat."

"So is mine."

He reached down and lifted her cock up as he lowered his mouth to it. As her cock entered his mouth she uttered a whispered "oh," caught her breath, and then moaned sweetly while she arched her back moving her cock further into his mouth.

He ran his tongue around the head of her cock then trailed his tongue down the underside of her rigid shaft. She began to move her hips rhythmically trying desperately to fill his mouth with her cock. He slipped his fingers down and found the lips of her pussy, wet with excitement. As he slipped his fingers inside of her she began to buck up and down against the rising tide of her orgasm.

Building in her like a tidal wave of passion, he sucked her cock and rubbed the inside of her vagina with dexterity. Suddenly, she exploded, thrusting her hips into a high arch and pushing his fingers out of her pussy. Her cock erupted in cum, filling his mouth and flowing down his chin. She screamed as she came, thrusting her body off the bed and then collapsing back in shudders. Beneath her butt the sheets were drenched with the juices that streamed from her in a burst of passion.

As she lay there quivering, she looked across to see him propped up on one elbow and watching her. He was wearing a goofy grin and the remains of her cum on his chin and lips.

"Oh my god Jason," she said trying to catch her breath, "that was amazing."

"Yeah, it was," he agreed laughing.

She used her fingers to wipe his face. "Is that my cum?"

"Yeah."

"All of it?"

"No, I swallowed some."

She pulled his face up to kiss him on the lips and lick her cum off his face.

"That was incredible. Jason, make love to me," she pleaded. "I want to feel you inside of me."

"Of course," he said as he smiled and nodded. He reached over and pulled a condom package off the nightstand. He sat up to open up the package when she placed her hand on his to stop him.

"You don't have to wear that if you don't want to."

"Why?" He held a condom wrapper in his hands and looked at her concerned.

"Because the doctor told me that I can't have children, because of how I am," she said her eyes filling with tears.

"Shush, sweetheart, it doesn't matter," he said sweetly as he tossed the condom onto the floor. Then he muttered softly, "We can always adopt anyway."

"What?" she asked smiling shyly.

"Nothing," he said kissing her on the lips and caressing her breast again.

But Rachel heard him nonetheless and she smiled to herself knowing what he really meant. That it wasn't important. That he loved her, enough to think about a future with her. And that was all that mattered.

She held him in her arms and felt his rigid cock slip between her thighs. She opened her legs to let him fill her pussy with his love. She felt him enter her. Without the condom she could feel every muscle and every vein and ridge of his stiff cock as he pushed inside of her.

She had put a dildo inside of her pussy before but it was nothing like this. She felt so full, so incredibly connected to him.

She felt him slowly begin to push and pull his cock inside of her. The sensations were indescribable. Her body was vibrating with an electrical charge that radiated from her head to her toes. She felt him begin to pick up speed rubbing the walls of her pussy faster and faster. She could feel the intensity of her passion growing with every stroke.

Suddenly her body exploded again, not as strong as the first time but equally intense. She wrapped her arms around him and dug her nails into his shoulders as she bucked and thrust her body against his.

Slowly the waves of passion subsided and she began to relax into a sense of euphoria as she floated sweetly along a river of bliss.

Jason snuggled closer and nuzzled against her breast. She wrapped her arms around him and pressed him against her chest. Her body still tingled from their lovemaking.

Suddenly it felt like her butt was wet. She sat up looking embarrassed and knocking Jason off the bed.

"Oh my god did I pee on the bed?" she cried out loud looking at the huge wet spot beneath her butt. "God, I'm so embarrassed."

"No sweetie," he replied climbing back into the bed, "you ejaculated the first time you came. It was spectacular. God, I wish I could come like that," he added with a look of wonder on his face.

"Really?"

"Yes, your body's wonderful, I'm so jealous." He leaned forward and kissed her on the lips.

She smiled shyly and blushed crimson then she looked up at him with a devilish smile. "Want to go again?" She reached over to tug on his growing cock.

The next day they booked a trip on a tour boat that offered scuba lessons. Rachel and Jason went diving for the first time and they adored it.

"I don't have to come back up for air!" she exclaimed joyfully. "This is so cool!" She rolled and twisted playfully like a sea otter.

"Tag, you're it," she said with a grin and she was off like a shot before Jason could catch her.

They spent the rest of the afternoon bobbing around coral heads and watching the world go by forty feet beneath the surface of the Caribbean Sea.

On the third and last evening of their trip Rachel had another surprise for Jason. It was officially his birthday and she had arranged a special dinner at a local restaurant. That night, their final evening of what was becoming a trip that neither of them would soon forget, they danced into the tiny hours of the morning.

After a quiet walk back to their hotel, they stepped out onto the terrace and opened their last bottle of wine. Their weekend adventure in the Bahamas was nearly over. Jason poured her glass and then his own. He lifted his glass to hers and looked into her lovely eyes.

"I love you Rachel."

"I love you Jason."

They kissed.

They embraced.

They made sweet and passionate love. And then they fell blissfully asleep.

=ELEVEN=

Jason raced home after his last class of the day. He knew that Rachel would be coming home soon and with what he had planned he wanted to be ready to surprise her by the time she arrived home. He threw his coat on the couch as he passed by heading for his bedroom. He sat at his dressing table, a gift to Jessie from Rachel just before she and Jason left for the Bahamas, and he opened up the box he left on the table from his shopping trip last night.

Inside was a new wig, long strawberry blonde hair flowed from the wig cap in subtle curls. He placed it on the wig stand and set about fixing his makeup. He'd been watching Rachel now for weeks as she worked her magic on him. He remembered the steps.

First the foundation; then follow that with a touch up of what needs fixing, then work on the eyes. He didn't want to rush things but he knew that time was short so he worked as fast as he could without messing it up. Tonight might be special if Rachel would agree to what he had planned.

A few minutes later, his makeup done, he pulled on his new wig and adjusted the cap to fit. He pulled on a new pair of thigh-high stay-ups and slipped on his new pair of Rachel Roi stilettos. This was the first time he wore them since he bought them. He remembered Rachel commenting that they looked dangerous and he was going to find out tonight if that was true.

About then he heard the familiar thump that told him that Rachel was home. He picked up his cellphone and texted her. 'Hey, Jessie's in the mood to chat, can she come over?' He waited to see her reply before he pressed on his fake nails. Texting with nails was just too hard without practice.

His phone chimed and he picked it up to see her message. 'Sure, I need to change. Ten minutes on the terrace?' she replied. He responded with a quick 'great, I have the wine,' and started to apply his nails.

Five minutes later, dressed in cutoffs and a slinky t-shirt that Rachel bought him in the Bahamas, Jessie emerged from the bedroom and sashayed across the living room to the kitchen to retrieve a bottle of white wine that was chilling in the refrigerator. He picked up two glasses and walked to his terrace door and slid it open.

Stepping over the low dividing wall he set the bottle and glasses on her table and settled down in one of the chairs, propping his feet up on the terrace railing and admiring the look of the shoes on his feet. They really did make his feet look sexy. He wondered if they would be enough of a hint for Rachel.

Rachel set her cellphone down and dashed into her bedroom. She wondered what he was up to? Jessie usually wasn't this forward. Most times she had to coax and cajole to get him to come over. Hmmm.

She pulled off her work clothes and tossed them on the bed then she pulled on a nice sundress and a pair of sandals. The weather was still nice out, even for the middle of October, and the chance to relax with a glass of wine after today sounded delicious, especially with Jessie as company.

As she stood in front of the bathroom mirror applying some makeup it suddenly hit her. She wants details! Of course! That little minx! A shy smile crossed her face. She decided to make her work for it.

Moments later Rachel slid open her terrace door to see Jessie admiring her new shoes. A new wig too! Hmmm, this could get interesting.

"Jessie, what a pleasant surprise."

"I haven't been around for a while, Rachel, I thought we'd catch up. How was the trip?"

"Lovely."

Jessie glanced over at Rachel. She twisted her mouth into a smirk. "Just lovely?"

"Yes, and fun, and exciting, and simply marvelous."

"You're teasing me aren't you?" Jessie scooted around in her chair around to look her in the eyes. "You know what I'm after and you're going to make me work for it aren't you?"

"What?" Rachel asked innocently as she looked off across the treetops swaying gently in the afternoon breeze. She paused a moment then smirked. "I can see that you're up to no good, that's what I see."

"You promised me details Rachel, I've brought wine to lubricate things if necessary," she replied with a devilish grin.

Rachel blushed crimson and downed the wine in her glass in one gulp.

"So, how was the trip?"

"It was marvelous."

"Details girl."

Rachel talked about the dinners and the fun they had shopping. "I made him go to a shoe shop with me. It was torture and I loved it. Plus, I even got him to pierce his ears."

"Yes, thank you for that, these are lovely earrings," Jessie purred as she flicked her dangling earring hoops. "But enough about shopping, what I want to know is did you do it?"

"It? No, I was on a holiday there was no time for I.T."

"Ha, Ha, very funny. Did you two make love?"

Rachel took a big breath let it out slowly into a gentle sigh then she whispered, "yes."

"And?"

"And again and again." The grin on Rachel's face hung off her ears as she leaned over and kissed Jessie on the cheek.

"Aw come on, you promised."

"No I didn't, but I will tell you that I started to fall in love with your brother the first day I met him. It grew and grew until I didn't think that I could be more in love. But I was mistaken. The moment I gave myself to Jason, completely and unconditionally, was the most beautiful moment in my entire life. You have a truly remarkable brother, Jessie, and I love him very much."

"And he loves you too." Jessie stood up and walked over to Rachel. She held out her hand. Rachel rose up into Jessie's arms and they held each other tightly.

Rachel wrapped her arms around Jessie's neck and leaned back with a gleam in her eye. "Now tell me why you're wearing those heels? You know that they just scream danger, don't you?"

"You know me too well, my dear friend." Jessie paused and looked into Rachel's eyes. "Jason wants to give himself to you, if you'll have him. He told me. Like you gave yourself to him; completely and unconditionally."

"You mean…"

"Yes."

"But, I've never done something like that before."

"That's okay, neither has he, so you can discover it together. He's waiting for you. Come to the terrace door in five minutes okay?"

Jessie took Rachel's hand and squeezed it gently then she stepped over the low wall divider that separated the terrace between the apartments and disappeared through the terrace door.

Jessie dashed into the bedroom and quickly pulled off the wig and shoes. Then she ran into the bathroom and wiped her makeup off with a face cloth to become Jason once again. He looked at himself in the mirror. This was the first time he was going to do something like this and it made him nervous. He knew there would probably be pain, Rachel's penis was pretty big, not huge but it wasn't tiny either.

The pain wasn't the issue; he was trying to mentally prepare himself for that. What really made him nervous was the fear that he might be pushing her too far, too fast. She might think he was some sort of freak and never want to see him again. The thought of that made his heart twist. He was beginning to realize just how much he loved Rachel and hopefully she loved him.

Jason closed the blinds on his bedroom windows and lit several candles on the dresser. He scanned the room quickly hoping that everything was perfect. Then there was a knock on the glass of the terrace door. He walked out of the bedroom to slide the door open and let her in. "Hi"

Rachel stood in the doorway and smiled sheepishly. "Hi. Jessie said you wanted to see me."

"I do." He took her hand and led her to his bedroom. She noticed the candles on the dresser and the window blinds drawn shut. The bed was turned down and there was a hint of lilac in the air. Jason released her hand as she entered his bedroom and he walked over to stand by his bed.

"Would you make love to me Rachel? Like I made love to you in Nassau?"

Rachel blushed crimson and smiled awkwardly. "Yes." Was all she could whisper, her breath was caught in her throat.

She walked towards Jason as he stood next to his bed. He looked so innocent, so beautifully innocent standing there, blushing crimson red and smiling meekly. She knew that from this point onward it was her turn to lead.

She also knew that she wanted this, to feel what it was like to take him, to explore her masculine side. She wanted to thrust into him wantonly and fill him with her seed. She could feel her cock stirring as she stood next to him. It was an arousal she had known but never this strongly. He was giving himself to her; he was offering something that she thought she would never experience.

Her eyes began to well up with tears as she

slowly began to undress him. Then she shook the tears away. She was going to be taking his virginity now; it was not the time to be feminine. Now was the time to take him and fill him with her love.

She unbuttoned his shirt and slipped it off his shoulders. She ran her hands across his chest and down to his cutoffs. She unbuttoned them and let them crumple at his feet. She stood back up to unbutton her dress but Jason moved her hands away.

"Let me," he said sweetly and he slowly undressed her. He slipped it over her shoulders and tossed it on the chair then he reached behind her to unfasten her bra. His hands were shaking and Rachel could feel his nervousness.

She leaned forward and kissed him gently on the lips then she hugged him. "I'll be gentle my sweet, I want you to enjoy this as much as me," she whispered softly in his ear.

He knelt down in front of her and placed his hands on her panties then lowered them down to fall at her feet. Her cock, now free from the confines of her lingerie, stood hard and proud against her stomach growing more rigid with anticipation. It pulsed with the throb of her heartbeat.

She reached down and lifted Jason to his feet. "Lie on your back my love, I want to watch your beautiful face as you give yourself to me."

He pushed the covers off the bed and then he settled into the pillows on his back to watch her.

She slipped on a condom he had placed there for her. She reached over and picked up a bottle of lube from the nightstand and lubed her cock slowly, seductively, watching him watch her. She moved her lithe body onto the bed. Her long hair was flowing around her head and shoulders; it shimmered in the rays of afternoon sunlight filtering through the blinds that masked his bedroom window.

She helped him move down the bed and she placed a pillow beneath his butt. She watched him open his legs to her. She was shaking she was so nervous and ecstatic all at the same time.

It was happening, she was going to do this. It was something she'd only dreamt about before this moment.

She crawled onto the bed and knelt between his legs. "You are so beautiful, my love." She coated his rosebud with lube and slipped one and then another finger inside of him. She watched him close his eyes and drift with the pleasure that she was giving him.

He clenched momentarily, reacting more to the chill of the lube than her invading fingers. Then he relaxed to her gentle touch, drifting as if buoyed by the pleasure of her touch in ways he has never sensed before. He felt open and vulnerable, yet at the same time he knew he was completely safe in her arms.

He felt her positioned her cock at his entrance. She rubbed against his anus for a moment then she pushed gently as she entered him slowly. He could feel every part of her as she moved past his outer ring.

Every ridge of her cock seemed to pulse and throb in tune with her heartbeat. His body stretched to accommodate her girth. He'd remembered what others wrote about their first time and he knew there would be pain but he was willing to accept that if it meant that he could be closer to her, to give himself to her as she had given herself to him.

He looked into her eyes as she pushed gently forward. She pulled back out and added more lubricant then she pushed back into him again going deeper this time. She continued slowly until her body pressed against him. She rested a moment and kissed him tenderly on the lips.

"Thank you my love, it feels so marvelous to be inside of you."

"I never knew how wonderful it would feel," he said as he wrapped his legs around her pulling her closer, urging her to go deeper.

She began to move in and out of him. Gently at first, then she picked up her pace as her passion soared. The feeling of being inside of him, the one she loved so deeply, was amazing. It was a moment that she would never forget.

Soon she was ramming into him, holding onto his hips as she drove deeper and deeper into him. Her passion soared and she erupted in him filling the condom inside of him with her seed.

Then they felt something warm and wet spread between their bodies as Jason came. He held her tightly against him, their bodies intertwined in passion and joy.

Rachel couldn't hold her emotions any longer. She began to cry. Huge teardrops ran down her cheeks and fell across his chest. She smothered him in kisses as she whispered to him. "I love you so much my sweet, my darling Jason. You fill my heart with such abundant joy."

=TWELVE=

Rachel came out of her bathroom wrapped in a bathrobe and scrubbing dry her hair. "Jason, Sarah called me this morning. She's having a barbeque in her back yard this weekend and we're invited." Jason stood in her kitchen making popcorn. It was Thursday night and that meant popcorn and corny movies on Netflix.

"Why did she invite us?"

"Because we're friends."

"Oh. Who did she invite, me or Jessie?"

"Probably Jessie." Rachel walked into her bedroom and rummaged around in her dresser for a clean pair of panties.

"Oh. That might be an issue."

"Why?" She found a pair and slipped them on.

"Because Jessie is kind of shy, especially vocally, you know?"

Rachel pulled on a t-shirt and a fuzzy pair of slippers and walked out into the living room. "Who cares? Sarah doesn't. She doesn't judge and neither do any of her friends, who are mostly women by the way."

"You mean there will be some guys there?"

"Yeah, sort of. I mean they were guys at one time. Now, not so much."

"Oh."

"I can't believe you're this upset." Rachel walked into the kitchen and kissed Jason on the cheek then she patted his butt.

"I'm not upset but I'm just…well, scared. Jesse has been someone who has been here just for you sweetheart. She gets nervous in public. You know that."

"Don't worry, Sarah likes you. And you already know one another. Besides, if anyone gives you a hard time she'll punch their lights out."

"What? How?"

"She used to box bantam weight in college." She took the bowl of freshly made popcorn and shuffled around the island counter to flop comfortably on the couch.

"She…what? You mean she's a…"

"Transsexual? Yeah, male to female. She told me last month she's still deciding on the big surgery. It costs a bundle and she's not ready yet up here either," she said pointing to her forehead.

"Oh…" Jason absentmindedly picked up two glasses of soda and walked around the counter to join her on the couch.

"So. Is Jessie going?"

"I suppose so. But you know I'll be a basket case beforehand."

"I know sweetie, but you'll do fine." She snuggled up against him and gave him a big kiss on the cheek then she settled down and grabbed the remote. "My night to pick," she said with a smirk. He rolled his eyes and sighed while she giggled.

=THIRTEEN=

Sarah lived in a cute little craftsman bungalow on the east side of town. It sat on a quiet cul-de-sac in a neighborhood infested with cul-de-sacs. The subdivision was one of those planned suburban sections where you could quickly get lost without a map or GPS on your cellphone.

As Jessie and Rachel walked up the path that led to Sarah's front door, Jessie noticed how nice the front yard looked. It was well landscaped and neatly trimmed.

Jessie wore casual slacks and a blousy shirt with her new black heels. Rachel wore a low cut red dress with that pair of Rachel Roi heels that she borrowed from Jessie.

"You're right," Jessie said with a huge grin, "those shoes are dangerous. I can't wait to get you out of them later tonight."

She smiled provocatively, teasing Jessie as she drew her fingers across his chin. "Sounds like fun," she purred.

There was a note on the door informing them to follow the signs and come around to the back. As they opened the side gate and walked into the backyard they could hear music playing in the background and lots of lively conversation.

"Hey, glad you made it!" shouted Sarah getting up from her lounge chair and setting her beer on the table beside it. "I was getting worried that you might have gotten lost."

"It is a bit of a maze. I will admit we were nearly lost a couple of times if it weren't for Jessie's GPS. This place is like the Bermuda Triangle."

"Yup, that's why I like it, it keeps out the riff-raff," Sarah grinned. She grabbed Rachel into a hug and gave her a peck on the cheek. Sarah turned to Jessie with a twinkle in her eyes. "Jessie thanks for coming."

Jessie nodded and smiled with a bit of a blush.

Sarah pulled him into a hug and whispered into his ear. "Relax girl, you're among friends here. Nobody judges."

"Thank you," Jessie offered shyly.

"Here, beer is in the cooler, wine is on the counter and burgers are almost ready to come off the grill. Howard, are they almost ready?" She looked at a huge hulk of a man towering over a grill at the corner of her patio.

He wore a leather vest covered with patches over a black t-shirt with the sleeves torn off. He was wearing faded black jeans out of which a large wallet chained to his belt nearly spilled from his back pocket. A bright red bandana pulled his hair back into a ponytail, which bobbed with his head as he moved to the music that must have been blasting into his earbuds.

"HOWARD!" Sarah shouted and everyone else laughed. Sarah looked at Rachel and Jessie then grinned. "He's half deaf from the pipes on that hog he rides and the other half is going quickly." She walked briskly across the yard and tapped Howard on his shoulder.

He turned with a huge grin and swooped her up into a big bear hug. His arms were a catalogue of tattoos, small, large, in full color and not. It was all rather crazy and the spectacle of Sarah swaying in his huge arms was quite amusing.

"Hi babe, what's up?" Howard asked with a toothy grin.

"I'll tell you what's up you ding-dong, we have more company." Sarah dropped to her feet and grabbed Howard's hand to drag him, if anyone could drag someone that huge, over to meet Rachel and Jessie. "Howard, this is Rachel Clark and Jessie Davies. Guys, this is Howard Hansen.

"Rachel leaned forward and extended her hand, which quickly became engulfed in his huge hand. Jessie was afraid that he might hear bones cracking but when he shook Howard's hand he was surprised how gentle he was.

"Glad to meet you, welcome to our home. I got to get back to the burgers. They're almost done. If I burn them I'll pay for it dearly," he said grinning and nodding towards Sarah. "She's tough."

Sarah leaned up and kissed him on the cheek then swatted his butt in the direction of the barbeque grill. "Make yourself comfortable. Everybody, this is Rachel and Jessie."

Several others shouted back. "Hello Rachel and

Jessie," and then they laughed.

Jessie began to relax a little. The party was filled with many of Sarah's clients and some of her friends, many of whom were transsexuals like her. The place was a little bit crazy, but maybe crazy was just what he needed.

Rachel mingled through the crowd, red solo cup in hand while Jessie, still feeling a bit shy, sought a chair by the pool to watch the festivities.

"Hi." A cute and curly redhead dropped down in the seat beside Jessie. She looked to be taller than he was, her long legs draped across the footstool in front of her chair.

"Hello." Jessie squinted into the afternoon sun and smiled at the girl next to him.

"I'm Janet, nice to meet you." She extended her hand with a welcoming smile.

"I'm Jessie, thanks, it's nice to meet you too."

"How do you know Sarah?"

"I'm just a customer, my friend Rachel took me there a couple of weeks ago."

"Don't you just love her store? I shop there every week. Shoes are my biggest weakness." She lifted her feet adorned with a pair of strappy sandals with five-inch heels. "Just call me Imelda Marcos!"

Jessie chuckled. "I love them too but on my budget I can't afford as many."

"What do you do?"

"I teach at the community college. How about you?"

"I work for a design firm downtown but I take classes at the community college. What do you teach?"

"English. Mostly composition. Occasionally I

get a chance at an intermediate writing course but not very often."

"Are you a writer?"

"Yeah, I try to be. Mostly pulp fiction stuff, romance and erotica. Have you ever written anything?"

"Oh God no, I'm a terrible writer, just ask my high school composition teachers. I'm surprised I even passed those classes. So have I ever read any of your stuff? Do you use your name or a pen name?"

"I've hardly published anything so far, I..."

"If you can find out her pen name you're a better person than me. I've known Jessie for six months and she still hasn't told me what it is. Hi, I'm Rachel." Rachel extended her hand and shook Janet's.

"Hi. Oh, are you two together?" Janet's face began to show signs of concern.

"Yes, but don't worry about it. It's nice to meet new people."

Jason got up and pulled another chair over for Rachel. "Did you come here alone?"

"Yeah, sort of. I came with my friend Brie; she's the tall blonde standing over there drooling over Howard's muscles. She knows better, Sarah will box her ears if she goes too far."

Rachel sat in her chair and adjusted the cushion. "No boyfriend?"

"Not lately. The last guy I was with didn't end so well. I sort of forgot to mention a few things and when he found out he was kind of pissed." Janet pulled back her hair and revealed a small scar on her temple near the hairline.

Jessie shook his head and sighed. "Shit, did you

press charges?"

"No, it's no use anyway. The courts don't want to hear about domestic disputes that include girls like us. So we just go home, lick our wounds, and start all over again." She shook her head as if clearing her head of negative thoughts.

"Hey, enough of that crap. Let's talk about something fun. I've got vacation time coming up, where should a single girl go? Any ideas?"

Rachel reached across and gave Jessie a big hug. "The Bahamas, definitely the Bahamas."

"We just got back a couple of weeks ago, can't you tell?"

"It was magical," Rachel added kissing Jessie on the cheek.

Janet laughed at their antics. "I see that. Tell me more."

"Janet! Come here, there's someone I want you to meet!" The tall blonde that Janet pointed to earlier was standing near a picnic table and talking to a couple of new arrivals. She motioned with her hands for Janet to hurry.

Janet stood up and grinned. "I guess I'm needed, sorry. Can I catch up with you guys later for the details?"

"Sure, wait a minute," Jessie said pulling out a pen and grabbed a napkin. "If we miss each other today, perhaps you can give us a call. We can talk over a cup of coffee sometime."

"That's very sweet, thank you, I'd love that. Bye." Janet turned and jogged towards her anxious friend still urging her to walk faster.

Rachel turned to kiss Jessie on the cheek again. "So, Ms. Popular, I guess I need to keep my eye on you."

"You have nothing to worry about sweetie, I'm totally smitten by you." She leaned in and returned her kiss. "Now, let's go try some of Howard's burgers, I'm starved."

As they walked towards the food table, Howard cranked up the music then grabbed Sarah for a dance. Apparently all the grillwork was over so now it was time to party.

It was kind of funny watching Howard, this hulk of a man, gliding across the dance floor working his salsa moves on his girlfriend Sarah. She looked a bit like Faye Ray in his arms. Not that Howard resembled a giant gorilla but he was huge. It was fun seeing everyone just enjoy themselves and for Rachel, she was glad to see Jessie relax more and enjoy herself too. She hoped that they could go out more often like this but she knew it would always be a battle to overcome her tendency to hide.

Watching Howard and Sarah salsa dance inspired Jessie to grab Rachel around the waist. She squealed as she hugged her. "Would you like to dance, gorgeous?"

"I'd love to, but let's eat first."

The afternoon passed into twilight and the party began to wind down. Rachel and Jessie said their goodbyes with promises to make the next barbeque whenever Sarah announced it. They wove their way out of Sarah's neighborhood with the expert guidance of Jessie's GPS phone and eventually climbed the three flights of stairs to their apartments.

Rachel leaned forward and kissed Jessie on the cheek as she fumbled with the keys to her apartment. "A glass of wine on the terrace my dear?"

"I'd love one, but I want to change first. I'll be out in a couple of minutes."

Rachel walked into her apartment and kicked off Jessie's shoes by the front door. She stopped in the bathroom to freshen up her makeup, then she walked into her kitchen and grabbed a bottle of chardonnay she had chilling in the fridge. Knowing how much they both enjoyed a glass of wine before bed, she put the bottle in to chill before they left for Sarah's.

She opened the wine and took two glasses off the shelf then she padded in stocking feet out through her terrace door.

A moment later Jason stepped out onto his side of the terrace holding a plate with slices of cheese and some savory crackers. He was wearing pajama bottoms and silky thin cotton t-shirt. He stepped gracefully over the dividing wall and joined Rachel at her table.

"Oh, you brought snacks, perfect."

"I had the munchies, I thought you would too." Jason sat the tray down on the table and poured himself a glass of wine. "So, how was the party?"

"Good, we had lots of fun and met a bunch of new people. What did you do while we were gone?"

Jason tried putting on a mock pout but half way through he grinned. "Sat around feeling lonely. I spent the evening watching old reruns of Friends."

Rachel grinned and popped a slice of cheese into his mouth. "Here, have some cheese, it'll make you feel better."

"Thanks."

Rachel munched on a few crackers and glanced sideways at Jason. Her mouth twisted into a wry grin. "Jessie got hit on by a couple of girls tonight."

"That's what she said." Jason looked off to watch the moon dance among the clouds.

"Some of those girls were very pretty. I know a lot of women who would love to look that good in those dresses."

"Yes, she told me that some of them were quite beautiful. She also told me about Howard."

"The Incredible Hulk? Yeah, he was very funny."

"Apparently a good dancer too."

"Uh-huh." Rachel watched the smirk play across Jason's face. It was obvious that he was toying with her. She was on a phishing expedition and he was going to make her work for the answers she wanted to hear. She decided that she might as well play along.

"So, have you ever thought about a relationship with a transsexual?" Rachel darted another glance across the table to watch his reaction to her question.

"Actually, I've led a pretty sheltered life up until I met you. Aside from Sarah, I've never met a transsexual before. And I didn't even know she was a transsexual until you told me."

"So, the question still stands, would you?"

"I think it's moot, my love. As long as I have you in my life, the rest of the world just doesn't matter." He turned to her with a gleam in his eyes. "Now about the shoes you wore tonight that just screamed 'take me'!"

He growled as he swooped her up into his arms and hugged her. She squealed and giggled as he carried her back into her apartment smothering her with kisses.

=FOURTEEN=

On the Tuesday following the weekend party at Sarah's, Jason called Rachel at work and asked her not to plan anything for Saturday.

"Why?"

"I want to go off on a little adventure, just the two of us. I promised you something when we were in the Bahamas and this is the last weekend we can do it before the season is over."

"Do what?"

"You'll see, it's a surprise. Wear something for the beach because that's where we're headed."

"The beach, huh? Okay. Hey, are you cooking tonight or am I?"

Jason could hear the excitement in her voice. "I am. How about something tropical and exotic."

"Did you say erotic?"

"Yup, that too. Bye."

Rachel heard the click on the phone. She set the receiver back into the cradle with a curious smile. What did he promise that weekend in Nassau that has to be done by this weekend?

She was so distracted as she tried to remember what he promised her that she didn't see or hear Wilson from accounting enter her office. "Earth to Ray, come in Ray."

Ray quickly tried to compose himself. "What? Oh, sorry, I was trying to work some puzzle out in my head. I didn't even hear you come in. What's up Fred?"

"My boss, Richter, wants to meet up with you about the server replacement order you sent up to accounts payable last week."

"What about it?"

"He says it's beyond the budget and wants to know how critical the issue is?"

"It'll be critical when the servers crash and he's back to an abacus and pencil while trying to keep his books."

"Ha! Should I tell him that?"

Ray stood up and moved around her desk to head for her office door. "No. Your boss doesn't have a sense of humor. It distracts him from the beans he's counting. Come on, let's go. I might as well do this now as later when things get really crazy."

Fred Wilson followed her out the door and down the hallway chatting in monotone about some other accounting issue. Ray's brain was beginning to fog over from the drone of his voice. It takes a certain kind of person to be an accountant, to stare at numbers all day and find joy in discovering a single digit out of place. Ray was not that kind of person, and she was thankful for that every time she ran into Wilson.

><><*

Jason was grilling something that smelled marvelous as Rachel, still dressed as Ray in shirt and tie, walked through her apartment door. She dropped her briefcase by the front door and walked out to the terrace. He was standing with his back to her swaying to music she couldn't hear as he had earbuds jammed into his ears. She walked up to him and, wrapping her arms around him, she hugged him tightly.

Jason pulled the earbuds out. "Hey beautiful."

"Yum, whatever you're cooking smells good." She hugged him again and she snuggled against his neck to take a big breath then let it out slowly. "Hmmm, so do you."

"I'm grilling pineapple and mango along with a spiced chicken glazed with a bourbon marinade. How was your day?"

"That sounds erotic like you promised." Ray let go of him and flopped down in a chair nearby. "Dreadful. You know, I spend all my time trying to keep that decrepit system they have running flawlessly. The moment I suggest that we need to spend some money to upgrade some of the older servers I get Richter on my back screeching about the lack of resources."

"Whoa, perhaps a glass of wine might help about now." Jason set his tongs down and walked into his kitchen to retrieve a bottle of wine and two glasses.

"Sorry, it's been a stressful day. It didn't start out that way. I got this cryptic call from my boyfriend about some special event he has planned for us on Saturday. Something about a trip to the beach and a promise made in Nassau?"

He stepped back out onto the terrace with two filled glasses of wine, one of which he handed to Rachel. "Is that so? What do you think it might be?"

"You're not going to tell me are you?"

"What? And spoil all your fun?"

"My fun? More like you're fun, you tease. Hmm this wine is good, which one is it?"

"Cocobon. It's new. A blend of reds with a hint of chocolate."

"Hmm, yummy." She took another sip. "So I should wear something for the beach, huh?"

Rachel set her wine down and stepped over the dividing wall that separated their two terrace sections. "Let me see what I've got." She opened her terrace door and disappeared inside.

She pulled off her tie and shirt as she walked quickly through her living room area towards her bedroom. She tossed her ball cap on the bed and dropped her trousers on the chair beside her dresser. Then she removed the ace bandage that helped her create the illusion that she was Ray and not Rachel.

She reached into the bottom drawer and pulled out a pile of swimwear. There were several one-piece suits; she tossed them into a pile on the floor. She might wear one on Saturday but this evening she had a different idea.

She pulled out a skimpy string bikini. It was bright yellow with tiny blue dots, the same one she wore for Jason in the Bahamas. It didn't cover much but just enough to tease the right response. She held the bra part against her breasts and glanced into the dresser mirror with a wicked grin. She quickly put the bikini top on then she pulled off her panties and slipped the bikini bottom up her legs. She reached down and tucked her cock back beneath the cloth and stood up to admire herself in the mirror.

To complete the look she dusted on a little smoky eye shadow, dabbed on some lip-gloss, and finished with a dash of mascara. As she began to walk towards the bedroom door she stopped. Jason was a sucker for high heels and she was standing barefoot. She turned with a devilish grin and opened her closet door. Inside she found a shoebox with a pair of six-inch sandals she bought from Sarah before she met him.

"He'll be like putty in my hands," she murmured as she stood up from adjusting her shoes and glanced one more time in the mirror.

She turned with a seductive smile and was out the door.

Jason was nearly finished with the chicken on the grill. He liked his new grill. It was small enough to fit comfortably on the terrace and yet large enough to handle a meal for the two of them. He pulled the last piece off the grill and onto a platter then he turned to shut down the burner when he heard Rachel's terrace door slide open.

He looked up to see a goddess sashay out through her door in dangerously high heels to strike a provocative pose on the terrace. The skimpy bikini, her long slender legs, and her shoes made Jason stop in his tracks. She was totally sexy, and from the ravenous look in her eyes she was on the prowl and he was her prey. "Hi," was all he could manage.

"Do you like?"

He shifted his hips a moment. "I think the tightness in my pants should tell you all you need to know."

She walked seductively towards him. As she neared him she began to unbutton his shirt. "Perhaps you can put that in the oven to keep warm. I feel like making you mine all of a sudden."

He grabbed the platter and dashed into the kitchen. He ran over to the counter and shoved the platter into the oven. He turned to see her standing right behind him. The ravenous look in her eyes was even stronger. She grabbed his hand and pulled him out the door, across the terrace and towards her apartment. As she backed him through her living room she finished unbuttoning his shirt and tossed it to the floor.

Next she almost tore his pants off. Her cock, the one she tucked so neatly beneath her moments earlier was emerging from the top of her bikini bottoms. Jason looked down. It was still growing. It looked larger than he remembered.

"You are mine tonight my love, all night long." She smiled wickedly as she maneuvered him towards her bedroom. "One of the cool things about being who I am is that I come like a woman, over and over and over again." She pushed him backwards onto her bed and stripped his underpants off in one stroke. "Since that first time you gave yourself to me I've craved this."

"Rachel my love, I am yours anytime you ask. I love to feel you inside me."

She reached across to the nightstand and opened the drawer to pull out a bottle of lubricant and a condom. "You know, one of these nights I want you to prepare yourself for me so I don't have to wear one of these."

"How about after dinner?"

"Really?"

He grinned at her sheepishly. "You did say all night, didn't you?"

She pushed two well-lubricated fingers into him in one thrust, he grunted and moaned as she moved them around to loosen him. He reached down and pulled on the stings of her bikini bottom to watch it fall away from her perfect ass. Her cock sprung out from it's confines long and hard, twitching in rhythm with her heartbeat.

"God, I want to be inside you now!"

He moved to spread his legs wider as she rolled the condom on her stiff cock. He held his arms up to embrace her as she moved forward to push her rod inside of him.

"Lord you fill me up, you're so huge. Deeper my sweet, go deeper."

He fell into the rhythm of meeting each of her thrusts as he locked his ankles around her, urging her to go deeper and harder. "Fuck me, God, I love it when you fuck me like this. Take me and make me yours."

=FIFTEEN=

The weekend couldn't come too soon for Rachel. She hated waiting for presents, particularly when she knew that they were going to be really special. When she was a child the weeks leading up to Christmas were always one big treasure hunt for her. Her parents knew she couldn't wait so they were especially diligent in hiding all her gifts. They knew full well if she found them she would open them immediately. But today's gift made her even more anxious because it was coming from the love of her life and he wouldn't even give her a clue.

Finally, it was Saturday morning and Rachel followed him down the stairs still peppering him with questions. He almost jumped down each flight he seemed so excited.

"I gave you tons of clues, you just weren't paying attention."

"I was so, your clues were too obtuse!" She stomped her foot on the landing and pouted. "Where are we going? Will we have to go far? Should we bring towels and suntan lotion? Which beach are we going to? Oh, this is so exasperating, what do you have planned?!

For each question he smiled enigmatically and refused to give her a direct answer.

"I told you it's a surprise darling, you'll just have to wait and see," he replied as he stood at the bottom of the last flight of stairs. He bounced up and down like a schoolboy anxious for the moment when she discovered his surprise. "We have towels and lotion already in the trunk of the car. Yes, and beach chairs too. Come on, we'll be late if we dawdle."

They drove off from the apartment building and headed out of town. They travel down a series of smaller highways and back roads because he didn't want her to guess too soon where they were going. Eventually, as they crossed a causeway over what at first looked like a huge lake, she began to realize that they were heading for the outer banks of North Carolina when she glanced at a sign as they started across. It said that they were crossing the Albemarle Sound.

"When did we cross into North Carolina?"

"A while ago."

Rachel watched another road sign pass by. It read Kitty Hawk five miles. "Kitty Hawk?"

"Well, you liked flying so much I thought I'd bring you to the place where it all began. We've just crossed over the Albemarle Sound causeway and we're headed for Kitty Hawk and the Wright brothers memorial."

"The Wright brothers, I remember learning about them in high school."

"Uh-huh. They came down here in 1903 to fly

the first airplane ever to take off and land under power. They believed that Kitty Hawk would be ideal place for their experiment."

"So we're going to visit a museum?" She sounded a bit disappointed. A museum could be interesting but she wanted an adventure.

"Of course. A flyer can't come to Kitty Hawk and not pay homage to the Wright brothers."

She thought about it for a few minutes. "Museums don't get you all that excited. What else do you have planned?"

He smiled at her cryptically. "You'll see."

She turned in her seat and crossed her arms with a huff. "Oh, you're such a tease!"

A half hour later he pulled up in front of a store. The sign above the entryway said Kitty Hawk Kites. "Come on, we have to sign in at the registration desk."

"You're not going to tell me a thing are you? Are we going to fly a kite?"

"Uh-huh, sort of." Jason was grinning from ear to ear as she sat in the passenger seat and pouted. "Okay, here's a hint. This is something I promised that I'd do for you when we were in the Bahamas."

"That's what you said over the phone, give me another hint."

"Okay. It has to do with flying. Now come on, we have a reservation for three o'clock."

"Flying? Here?"

They went inside to the front counter where they registered with an instructor named Carl.

"Hi, are you both taking lessons?"

"Not today, just my girlfriend Rachel. She told me a month ago how much she really wanted to try this."

Carl grinned and extended his hand to Rachel. "Great, you're going to love it! Come on, we need to check a few things and then we'll head out across to the launch area."

Rachel turned and looked at Jason. "Launch area?" Her eyes twinkled with excitement. "What did you sign me up for?"

"You said you wanted to learn how to fly didn't you? Well this will be you're first lesson."

Carl peeked his head around the corner and motioned for them to follow him to the fitting rooms. "We need to fit you into a harness Rachel. The sand is soft but it still makes a hard landing if you're not strapped in to the kite.

"Come on, let's follow Carl. Then we need to head up to that big dune over there." Rachel followed his arm and looked out the window at a huge mountain of sand. Her eyes grew large as she watched someone literally jump off the side of the hill and glide several hundred feet downhill.

She squealed as she wrapped her arms around his neck and kissed him. Jason grabbed her hand and led her around to the fitting room.

"Okay Rachel, have you ever flown before?"

"Only as a passenger."

Carl nodded and smiled. "Great. That's actually a good thing. We've had pilots try this before and it can get pretty crazy. They're reflexes tell them if you pull back you go up. But with kites it's the opposite. Pulling back sends you right into the sand, not so good."

Rachel nodded as Carl began to go over the basics of flying a hang glider while they slowly trudged up the mountain of sand.

"We'll do the first flight together as a tandem. Then as you get the feel of it you can solo, okay?" It was all a bit overwhelming, but Jason could see that she was jumping for joy.

Rachel nodded again then glanced over to Jason, her eyes sparkled with excitement. He was standing in an area cordoned off for spectators and grinning like a Cheshire cat. She couldn't believe that she was going to fly, not in some big aluminum tube but soar like a bird with a huge wing lifting her up into the air. She glanced again at Jason as the hang glider crew began to clip her into the tandem harness on the huge kite.

Carl positioned himself on the left and motioned for Rachel to step beside him. "The tandem kite is larger than the solo kite so don't be intimidated by it's size. The control is relatively simple. You push the control bar away from your body to go up, pull back to go down. Lean left to go left, lean right to go right. The kites are pretty rugged so it's no big deal if we crash. Other than a little sand in your face, you'll be fine. Don't worry, it happens all the time."

"Just my pride will take a beating."

Carl laughed as he clipped the remaining rings of his harness onto the kite. "So did mine the first time I tried this. I think you'll do great."

She nodded at Carl and watched as he lifted the kite up from the ground. This was really going to happen! She was going to fly. Her heart was racing. She couldn't believe how much her life had changed in the few short months that she's known Jason. She never would have believed that a simple little prank, painting her neighbor's toenails red, would lead to this. Here she was standing on top of a huge mountain of sand, strapped to an enormous cloth wing, and about to leap off into another amazing adventure. My God she loved that man.

Carl helped one of the assistants adjust her harness. "We're all set. Are you ready?"

"As I'll ever be."

He lifted up the control bar of the kite and nodded to his assistants holding the outer ends. The wind caught the sailcloth and the material fluttered. "I'll get us started then it's up to you. I'll be here if you need me, okay?"

"Okay." Rachel gritted her teeth and grinned. She wanted to stamp her feet and scream she was so excited. Instead she put a death grip on the control bar and waited as Carl pushed the bar forward into the wind and they began to lift off. Up and up they went as the wind swirled around them pulling the kite higher off the mountain of sand.

Carl pulled back slightly on the control bar and they began to move forward. Rachel, in spite of her excitement, kept a close eye on how Carl was handling the kite. She wanted to know how he moved the control bar and how the kite responded to his body position. As the wind raced past her ears, Rachel looked down to see the ground quickly move away from her feet. Her eyes opened wide as she watched the kite soar into the sky.

Below her, standing in the observation area, she saw Jason watching them soar into the sky. They quickly moved down the mountain lifting almost a fifty feet above the sand. Flying with them, laughing seagulls circled the strange delta shaped object that lifted higher into the sky. They swooped in curious then squawked as they flapped away.

Carl shouted over the rush of wind. "You think you've got it?"

Rachel nodded and she felt Carl relax his grip on the control bar. "She's all yours. Try to go a little higher."

She pushed against the control bar and she felt her body move backwards as the nose of the kite lifted higher in the air.

Carl grinned at her. "That's it, now let's bank a bit to the right."

She shifted her body to the right and felt Carl move with her. The kite dipped its wing and slowly moved to the right.

"That's right but not too much. We can pitch pole this thing if we go too far. Every movement should be gentle, sudden movements can get you into trouble quickly."

She shifted back to center and she felt the kite move back towards the bottom of the hill, which was quickly approaching. Carl took over the controls. Rachel watched as he gracefully held the control bar then pushed it forward at the last moment to flair the kite skyward into a stall and let them land on their feet.

"Fantastic! You did an excellent job." Carl reached over and patted Rachel on the back. "Are you ready to go again?"

"Can I?"

Rachel trudged slowly back up the mountain of sand. As she neared the top she shouted to Jason. "You have got to try this!"

"Next time, sweetheart, today is your day."

She made three more attempts that day. On her first solo flight she drove the nose of the kite into the sand twenty feet from where she lifted off. Even with sand falling out of her swimsuit she stood grinning like a kid on Christmas morning. Jason was flying as high as she was watching her have the time of her life.

On her second solo attempt she flew clear down the mountain to land like a pro at the bottom of the hill. She flared the kite into a stall at just the right moment and she touched down like she'd been doing this for years.

"Your girlfriend is a natural," said Jake, another hang gliding instructor.

"Yes she is," Jason said with a huge grin.

That night they checked into a quaint little bed and breakfast place in Manteo, just down Highway 12 from Kitty Hawk. Rachel collapsed on the bed as Jason closed their bedroom door. She rolled over and pulled him into a hug. "You beautiful, wonderful man, do you know how much joy you've given me today?"

He just beamed. "Come on beautiful, let's get in the shower and make love under our own personal waterfall."

Later, in the afterglow, Rachel rested next to him and playfully teased his nipples. "What are your plans for Christmas?"

"Whoa, that was out of left field."

"Sorry, I just remembered that the company sent around a flyer on Friday trying to finalize a day for the annual Christmas party. I know it's early but they like to plan these things out well in advance. So, what are you planning to do for Christmas?"

"It sounds like you have a party to attend."

"Yes, and everybody wants to meet you. But you will have to be dressed as Jessie."

"Why? Can't I just go as your long lost cousin?"

"Ha! No. The head of the firm wants to meet you. I've told him all about you. And then Oscar my supervisor wants to thank you for taking care of me that time when I got beat up."

He rolled his eyes and groaned. "How will you be dressed?"

"I'm going as Ray of course."

He groaned again as he sat up in bed. "Dressed, huh? Does that mean I have to wear a dress?"

"It would be nice, but you don't have to. I suppose we could find you a women's business pantsuit that might look okay if you want. Then again, I don't think you have the hips for it."

"I don't know. You know I would probably look like a gorilla in drag, sweetie."

"Do you want to bet on it?"

"No, because every time you have that look in your eyes, I lose."

"Bet me."

"What's the prize?"

"If I win you come to my Christmas Party dressed to the nines. Evening gown, heels, makeup, the works."

"And if I win?"

"You can wear jeans," she replied with a smirk. "But you know you're not going to win don't you?"

"Yup. By the way, I'm officially inviting you to attend my Christmas party at the college as Rachel. The Dean wants to meet you. I'm supposed to be presenting some kind of faculty awards during the evening so it's not something I can get out of."

"When is it?"

"Probably the same night as your party at the office. I think the world coordinates these things to make it difficult for people like us.

"How are we going to do that?"

Jason smiled roguishly with a shrug. "We'll find a way, we always do."

=SIXTEEN=

The next week on Wednesday, Jason returned to his office after his first morning class. He needed to pick up a few books to reference in his Literature class coming up.

Janet Tabor knocked on his office door. She was the cute and curly redhead who Jason met dressed as Jessie at Sarah's barbeque party the previous weekend. "Hi, remember me?"

Jason's cheeks immediately flushed crimson red. "Ah, oh, sure, Janet right? Hi. Would you like to sit down?" Jason glanced both ways down the hall hoping that none of his colleagues had seen the cute little redhead bounce into his office.

"Thanks." She looked around as she sat and then turned back to smile at Jason. "Nice office."

"Thank you." Jason tried not to look her in the eyes. He couldn't help it. Janet knew about his alter ego, Jessie. If word got out his life would be a disaster, let alone his career. The last bastion of stubborn conservatism in the public sector is academia. University professors don't walk those hallowed hallways in five-inch stilettos for a reason.

"Did I come at a bad time?"

"No, no. I'm just a little surprised. I guess I didn't expect that you would visit me, or so soon."

Janet paused and looked at Jason fidgeting behind his desk. She dropped her head with a wry smile and glanced back up to catch him looking at her. Worry was etched across his face. "Don't worry Professor Davies, we girls need to stick together. You're secret is safe with me. Besides, if I ever blabbed, Sarah would ban me from her shop and that would be beyond horrible."

Jason laughed a nervous laugh and relaxed a tiny bit. "So what can I help you with?"

"Well, actually I came to meet you and to talk about the Bahamas. You guys went on and on about your trip last weekend so I wanted to learn more. My girlfriend Brie kept me occupied for the rest of that day with those two hunks that she thought were gorgeous. But let me tell you, the package might have been pretty but the contents were not. Those two were as dumb as a box of hammers."

Jason laughed. "A box of hammers, I have to remember that. As for our trip, I can't right now; I have a class in ten minutes." He glanced quickly at his watch. "Make that eight minutes. But here," he pushed a piece of paper and a pen towards her, "write down your cell number so I can text you after I've had a chance to talk to Rachel. Maybe we can grab dinner or something."

She scribbled her number on the scrap of paper and slid it back to him. "That would be fantastic! I wanted to see her again too."

Janet slung her backpack over her shoulder and extended her hand to him. Jason took her hand and gave it a firm shake. She leaned forward and whispered. "You make a very handsome man too, by the way."

Jason blushed crimson again and smiled meekly.

She giggled as she waved at him then she stepped through the doorway. "I hope to see you later tonight." She left his office and walked down the hall.

As she walked away, one of Jason's colleagues, Mike Allen stepped out of his office. He looked up to watch her walk down the hallway. Then he walked up and leaned against Jason's office door, letting out a low whistle. "Man how do you score all the gorgeous chicks when all I do is wash up on the beach like drift wood?"

"What do you mean?"

"Don't give me that. What about that hottie that just left your office? What is it about English Literature types that attract all these gorgeous babes while I stare out at a sea of blank faces? Introduce me."

"She's a special girl, Mike. She's in a fragile place right now and I don't want her hurt anymore than she already is."

"She just got dumped, huh?"

"You could say that."

Mike shook his head. "Who would be stupid enough to dump a beauty like that?"

"Like I said, she's a special girl." Jason pushed his fist into his other hand. "Her ex-boyfriend didn't exactly like her specialness."

"What? He beat her up?"

"Yeah."

'That's fucked up. And I suppose you think I might do that?" He shook his head again, this time in disbelief. "I'm not like that man."

"Mike, some guys get really crazy when they find out about a girl like Janet."

"Janet. That's her name, huh? God is Gracious."

"What?"

"It's the meaning of her name, Janet. God is Gracious. It's an old English name. My cousin took the name of Janet when she transitioned. That's how I know about it. She looked long and hard for a name that she thought suited her and she decided on the name Janet."

"Huh?"

"That doesn't bother you does it?"

"What?"

"That my cousin was born a different gender?"

"No, of course not."

Mike sighed. "Good. It does some guys, I'm glad you're not one of them."

"Actually, the whole gender issue is more common than most people think. I lot more people than the general public are aware of are intersexed in one form or another. Then there are the people who feel that they were born in the wrong gender, like your cousin. They want to change it but don't for a lot of reasons. It's just that with social pressures, most people don't want to face the ugly side of that decision. So they keep it too themselves, bury it deep inside. Your cousin is one of the brave ones."

Mike nodded and smiled. "Yes, she is, very brave indeed."

"What was her name before she transitioned?"

"Stephen. She didn't like Stephanie. She wanted

to be a whole new person."

"What did you think while she was going through the change?"

"I thought she was the most courageous person in the world. Her parents totally disowned her; all of her so-called friends told her she was a perverted freak. I was the only one in the family, aside from her grandmother, who supported her. She came to live with me for a couple of months before she went off to college. And she always stayed with Grandma or me for holidays while she was in college."

"Did she have the full sexual reassignment surgery?"

"Not yet but I think it's the plan. She's saving up money right now and she's going through a lot of testing and counseling."

"Do you ever see her?"

"We Skype sometimes. She lives on the west coast near Portland. She's married with two kids from her husband's previous marriage. She's a soccer mom and a member of the PTA living the good life in suburbia. I think she's great."

Jason paused a moment. He knew he might be taking a risk introducing Janet to Mike without at least giving her a chance to choose whether or not she wanted someone new in her life. But his heart told him that there was a reason why Mike opened up like he did.

"Mike, I'll talk to her. I know she's planning a trip to the Bahamas just to recuperate from her last boyfriend so I don't know if she wants to see anyone yet. But if she wants to meet you, I'll help."

"Really? I love Nassau."

"Yeah, so do I. I'll let you know what she says

soon, okay?"

Mike got up and walked to the door. He turned and smiled at Jason. "Thanks, and you're late to class." Then he was out the door and down the hall.

"Damn it!" Jason bolted out of his office and raced down the hall towards his classroom.

=SEVENTEEN=

That evening, Jason walked out onto the terrace after he dropped his briefcase near the front door of his apartment. Waiting for him was a nicely chilled glass of Chardonnay, and his girlfriend dressed in casual slacks, a white shirt and tie. "Lovely." He gulped the wine down and held out his glass for another.

"If you're going to gulp it I'll just pour you a glass of water."

He jiggled his glass and put on his best puppy dog sad face. Rachel's heart melted and she poured him another. "Why the sudden rush towards drunkenness?"

"Not drunkenness, sweetheart, just a desire to take the edge off the day. It's been a rather long one, with interesting moments along the way."

"How so?"

"Well, for one, I ran into Janet Tabor this afternoon."

The color ran out of Rachel's face. "Janet? You

mean the Janet we met at Sarah's party, Janet?"

"Yup. She knocked on my door and wanted to talk about the Bahamas. Needless to say I was a basket case inside. I didn't know what to do or say. Then she told me not to worry, that my secret was safe with her."

"Whew, that's good. Did you talk about our trip?"

"There wasn't time, I had to get to class so I asked her to wait for a text from me to see if you were willing to meet her for dinner. It would be just the three of us."

"Sure, when?"

"Tonight? There's a little Mexican place on Roberts Street that's pretty good."

"Okay, but I need at least an hour. My day wasn't any better than yours I guess."

"What happened?"

"You know that storm that blew through here this afternoon?"

Jason nodded. He remembered walking from one classroom building to another when the storm started. By the time he made it to class he was drenched.

"Well, lightning must have struck nearby because half of our servers went down. The older ones, the ones I wanted them to replace last month with better surge protection." She shook her head slowly. "I was able to patch a few holes but there will be a lot to do tomorrow."

Jason lifted her left foot and pulled off her shoe. He began to rub the arch of her foot.

"Oh my God that feels so good. My boyfriend spoils me rotten and I love it. So did you text Janet?"

"I will now. How about we meet her at seven?"

"Sound good, I can get a shower too. After you text her do my other foot, please." She looked at him with a cute pleading smile and batted her eyelashes.

Jason sent off a quick text to Janet and she replied almost immediately. "She says that sounds great. Oh, which reminds me, I had another interesting moment this afternoon right after she left my office."

Jason related his meeting with Mike. As he explained what was said he could see her expression cloud with concern. She's lived through bigotry before and he knew she wouldn't wish it on her worst enemy.

"I think he'll be all right. He has a cousin, also named Janet, who transitioned male to female before she went to college. He told me she's married now and living the good life, as he put it, on the west coast. I asked him what he thought about it and he told me he thought she was the most courageous person he had ever met."

"He said that?"

Jason nodded and smiled. "I think I'll tell Janet about him. Then it will be up to her to decide if Mike is someone she wants to have in her life."

Rachel nodded lost in thought as Jason resumed his assault on her sore feet. So many times in the past people she thought would accept her for her uniqueness, didn't. And sometimes their response was violent. She remembered Jason healing her back from the last guy who didn't like surprises.

Jason pulled her into his arms and kissed her. "I'm not going to let anything happen to Janet if that's what you're worried about. Besides, Mike knows me. If he does something wrong, I'll get Howard to fix it for me."

"Sarah's Howard? If he fixes it, it could be permanent."

"I know. Come on. If you're going to get a shower we need to get going."

=EIGHTEEN=

Jason pulled into the parking lot at Mi Casita's Mexican restaurant and parked his car. "Do you think she's waiting for us?"

"I don't know, we did take longer in the shower than I expected." Rachel leaned over and kissed him on the cheek. "But then, I didn't expect such a lovely blow job to help me take the edge off the day."

"Mmm, you tasted good too." He opened his door, got out, and together they walked to the restaurant entrance hand in hand.

"Hi, we're meeting someone, Janet Tabor?" The hostess at the door nodded and led them through a maze of booths and tables over to a booth on the far wall.

Janet stood up as they approached. In heels she was slightly taller than Rachel. Her curly red hair was pulled back into a ponytail and she wore a pretty print floral dress that subtly revealed a beautiful set of breasts above a slender body with gentle feminine curves. "I'm so happy to see you guys, I was anxious and got here early." She reached forward and hugged Rachel first. Then she turned and hugged Jason. "Thank you both for meeting me, but I was hoping to see Jessie again."

Rachel smiled gently and then leaned forward to speak softly. "Jessie is very shy and doesn't come out in public much."

"Just to Sarah's, and even then she was a nervous wreck."

Janet smiled sweetly. "I understand, but I did enjoy meeting her so I hope that I will see her again."

Rachel glanced at Jason as he nodded and smiled. "Me too."

"As you probably can understand, outside of Brie, I don't have many friends. It's so hard to meet people you can trust enough to be open without fear of judgment."

Jason unzipped his coat and pulled it off. "I know what you're saying Janet, just this afternoon one of my colleagues surprised me by talking about his cousin who transitioned."

"Really?"

"Yes, in the world of academia, being candid about something like that is rare. Janet, I wanted to talk about this later but..."

Janet looked from Jason to Rachel bright eyed and excited. "What?"

"Look, I just met you and I really don't know much about you. I was thinking that given your recent experiences that meeting someone new before you've had a chance to get your life back in order might be pushing things."

"Are we talking about the guy who poked his head out of his door when I left your office this afternoon?"

"Maybe, what did he look like?"

"Well, I only glanced in his direction when I left but I'd say tall, maybe your height, sandy blonde hair and a bushy mustache."

"That's the one. His name is Mike Allen."

"He's cute."

Jason spent the next few minutes replaying the conversation he had with Mike after Janet left. About how Jason felt that Janet was in a difficult place right now and it might be too soon to meet someone, especially someone she doesn't know.

"He thinks I'm a hottie, huh?" Janet blushed as she grinned mischievously. "I know, I know, I'll behave. But it's kind of nice to hear that someone you don't know thinks your hot, right?" She glanced at Rachel who smiled demurely.

About then a waitress arrived with chips, salsa, and water. She asked them if they wanted anything else to drink but all of three of them just wanted water. "Would you like to order now or do you need a couple of minutes?"

Rachel smiled. "Just a minute or two, please."

The girl nodded and left as they buried their noses in the menus. A moment later Janet peeked over the top of her menu. "Yes."

Rachel looked up at her curiously. "Yes, what?"

"Yes, I'd like to meet him."

"Are you sure?"

"Uh-huh. Something inside is telling me that I'm supposed to meet him so, yes, I'd like that."

Rachel glanced at Jason then looked back at

Janet. "Jason told me that if anything happened he'd ask Howard to fix it for him."

"Howard? Sarah's Howard?" She laughed and reached over to take Rachel's hand. "Howard looks like he could break somebody in half but he has a heart of gold. I suppose if he was really pissed off..."

Jason laughed. "I got the same impression. But don't worry; I feel the same way about Mike. I've only known him for a couple of months, but I like him. He's a good guy and I hope it works out for you two."

A moment later the waitress returned. They placed their order and she was off to bring them more chips and salsa. The rest of the meal was filled with laughter as Jason and Rachel retold their stories again about their adventures in the Bahamas.

Rachel dabbed her mouth with her napkin. "When are you thinking about going?"

"I can't get off work until almost Christmas, so I suppose it will be then."

"Well, you'd better make your reservations soon because Christmas is a busy time down there."

Janet nodded and dipped a chip into the salsa. "Can I hang out with you guys again sometime?

"Sure, we'd like that."

Jason nodded as he picked up his fork. "There's a play opening up in a couple of weeks at the college. Maybe we can do a double date."

"That sounds great! Besides, I have to see it for my theatre appreciation class. Now it will be fun too."

Outside, in the parking lot, there were hugs all around.

Janet just beamed as she hugged and kissed Rachel on the cheek. "I'm so glad I met you guys at

Sarah's. You're both the best." She turned and hugged Jason with a peck on his cheek. "Maybe we can get together sometime, just us girls, for coffee or something."

Jason smiled shyly. "Maybe."

After they returned to their apartment building, Jason and Rachel went for a walk through a quiet park nearby. In the center of the park was a small pond surrounded by clusters of day lilies. The placid water reflected the moonlight that filtered through the trees. They sat for a moment quietly and listened to the night sounds then Jason pulled out a small narrow box and handed it to her.

"What's this?"

"A little memento, something to remember your trip to Kitty Hawk."

Inside was a delicate silver bracelet with tiny airplane propellers dangling from the chain.

"Jason...I don't know what to say. This is so beautiful."

"I was thinking that tonight I want to prepare myself for you again. I really loved the feeling of you inside me without a condom when we did it that way last week."

"I'd liked that too. Maybe we can do this together; I've never given myself to anyone that way before. So you like it when I make you mine?"

"I adore it. The feeling of you possessing me as I totally submit to you is enchanting. Your thrusts inside of me are so gentle yet so demanding. I feel so connected to you; it's a sexual high that I've never felt with anyone before I met you. That first time was incredible and then, last week, when you took me in that sexy bikini, that was awesome. You filled me with so much joy, I was high for days after that."

He leaned over and kissed her lips. "I've listened to men talk about it, submitting to their wives. Most of the talk centers on the machismo fear of loosing the dominant position in a relationship. But your gift of loving me that way, of lifting me up to an ecstasy that I've never felt before, it's a gift of pure love. There is no dominance or submission, just lovers, sharing themselves in bliss. You make me feel loved beyond measure."

Rachel wrapped her arms around him and kissed him passionately. "I love you so much. You are the most wonderful man in the whole world."

=NINETEEN=

"Hey, that was Sarah." Rachel walked out onto the terrace with the bottle of red wine she opened earlier. "She just invited us to her house for Halloween."

Jason sighed a little then he looked up from the papers he was grading. "You know, I only ever agreed to be Jessie to shop for shoes with you. It was just supposed to be between us."

She leaned over and kissed his forehead then sat down on the edge of the lounger next to him. "Oh pooh, you had fun at Sarah's the last time. Come on, admit it."

"Okay, I admit it was fun, but I was a nervous wreck the whole time."

"And meeting Janet was great too, wasn't it?

"Of course. I don't know...I just feel like it's beginning to spin out of control and it scares me."

She stood up and gazed into his beautiful eyes. "You are so cute when you're like this. I just want to wrap my arms around you and snuggled all night."

She kissed his cheek and nuzzled up under his chin. "Besides, weren't you the one going off about the corrupt social construct?"

He dropped his head and nodded. Then he set his stack of student papers aside and wrapped his arms around her. He couldn't help it, he was putty in her hands and she knew it. Suddenly a frightening thought occurred to him. "Rachel, if it's Sarah's party then Janet will be there. And if that's the case, then there's a good chance that she'll bring Mike. I'm just not prepared to face one of my colleagues dressed as a woman, even if it's only heels and makeup."

"Why not? It's a Halloween party; you could go as Lady Gaga."

"Be serious. Besides, I said no dresses, right? I'd look like a..."

"I know a gorilla in drag. No you won't."

"No dresses, okay?"

Rachel's eyes sparkled with mischief. "Wait, I know. You can go as Jason."

"Really, you think I could go as me?"

"No silly, as Jason, the one in the horror movies, that Jason."

"Oh...okay, yeah, that might work." Jason held up his hands and looked at them closely. "Is that the guy with the long knives in his hands?"

"No sweetie, that's Freddy Kruger. Jason is the one in the hockey mask."

"A mask? That's even better."

"And a machete." She was getting more excited about the prospect of dressing up for Halloween.

Jason was beginning to discover just how much she enjoyed this holiday.

"Wait, I think a chainsaw would be better, don't

you? We can mix things up a little, why not?"

"Where are we going to find a chainsaw?"

"My nephew has one, it's a toy, his dad bought him one when he was five. I'll call this evening and see if we can borrow it."

"How are you going to be dressed?"

She raised an eyebrow with a devilish grin. "As one of your scantily clad victims, of course."

"How do you know so much about these movies?"

Rachel looked innocently over her shoulder then turned and winked. "Secret pleasure, they make me laugh, they're so over the top and ridiculous."

"But all that blood."

She giggled as she leaned back and caressed his cheek. "Wait till you see the costume I have in mind."

"Huh?"

The afternoon before Sarah's Halloween party Rachel reached through the passenger door of Jason's car with a plastic drop cloth. "Here, put this plastic sheeting over the front seats."

"Why?"

Rachel grinned devilishly. "Do you want fake blood all over the upholstery?"

"Oh, okay, good idea."

"That looks good. I'm going to get dressed; I'll meet you in your living room in fifteen minutes, okay?" She scampered up the three flights of stairs to their apartments.

Jason remembered costume shopping with her the other day. They went to several thrift stores until she found the right dress. It was a spaghetti strapped cocktail dress that hugged her curves like a kidskin glove. If it wasn't for the garish color and frayed hem, he was going to suggest she keep it for a night out. She bought a pair of torn work pants and a grease stained white shirt for his costume. Then they stopped at her brother-in-law's house and picked up the toy chainsaw.

"Perfect." She pulled the trigger and the toy growled, trying to sound like a chainsaw but failing miserably. Still the effect would be enough to get a laugh and that's what she was going for.

She spent the next day or so hacking up her costume with a pair of scissors and a butcher knife. He was amazed at her enthusiasm. When she finally put it on, it was the sexiest thing she'd ever worn. Except for that white dress she wore in the Bahamas. Her beautiful breasts were now barely covered, her slender waist showed in several places where large chunks of the dress were sliced away. And the hem was torn so badly it struggled to cover her thighs. After she mixed and applied the fake blood recipe she found on the Internet, she slipped on that infamous pair of white sandals, the ones she first put on Jason's feet so many months ago and she walked into Jason's living room. She slowly twirled in front of him. "What do you think?"

"That outfit you have on is totally sexy. I'm not sure we're going to make it to Sarah's at this rate."

"Hmm." She leaned forward and kissed him lightly on his nose. "After the party is over my love, I'll be yours to ravage like the monster you are." She giggled sweetly and brushed her hand across his chin lightly tracing her nails across his jaw.

"God you make it hard for me to resist you."

"I can see something else that's hard too. Should I help you with that?"

She pulled him onto the tiled floor of the kitchen and licked his cheek, smearing fake blood all over his costume. She giggled as she tugged at his belt then lowered his pants to reveal his stiff cock throbbing with anticipation.

He moaned gently as she took him into her mouth, pre-cum was dripping from the head of his cock. "God you taste good," she murmured between strokes. Her mouth worked wonders on his raging hard-on. He was so turned on it only took a few more strokes and his knees were buckling under the velvet touch of her agile tongue.

"You have me totally under your spell, you know that don't you?"

She giggled shyly and nodded.

"How about I return the favor?"

"Oh no sweetheart, I want to save that for later. Then I'm going to fill you up, over and over again." She giggled again and curled into his arms wrapped around her shoulders, the fake blood smeared across both of their cheeks and faces.

When Jason turned into the cul-de-sac where Sarah lived they could already hear the bass thump from the sound system that Howard probably installed that afternoon. It was loud enough to rattle the windows on the neighbor's houses.

"I hope they invited the whole neighborhood, cause nobody's going to sleep through this."

They walked up to Sarah's front door and saw the familiar sign pointing them to the backyard gate. They walked through the gate as a rather huge hairy man in a skimpy swimming suit did a cannonball off the diving board into the pool.

"Oh, I forgot about the pool." The splash sent a tidal wave of water rushing to all four sides as others laughed and scrambled to get out of the water.

Rachel laughed as Howard swam to one side of the pool with a huge grin on his face. "Now that's a cannonball," he shouted.

"I didn't dress for the pool."

"Oh don't worry sweetie, I can't go in either, it would ruin my costume."

"What little there is of it."

"Exactly. Oh, there's Janet and that must be Mike. Come on."

Janet and Mike stood laughing as Howard, emerging from the pool and holding a super soaker water gun as he chased Sarah across the backyard.

Mike had his arm around Janet's waist as she fell into his arms laughing. He looked over her shoulder as Rachel and Jason walked up. "Hey there, glad you could make it. Nice costumes by the way. Oh wait, I get it, Jason from the movies Jason. Very clever."

Jason grinned sheepishly. "It was Rachel's idea. Mike, this is my girlfriend Rachel Clark. Rachel, this is Mike Allen, one of my colleagues from school.

Janet leaned over and gave Jason a big hug. She whispered in his ear. "Nice way to sidestep the gender issue Jessie, I like it." She turned to Rachel and laughed at her body covered with slashes and blood. "I love you babe, but you're not getting any hugs from me tonight."

Rachel stood apart from them and opened her arms wide. "Aw, come on, give me some sugar!"

"Nope, not going to happen." Then Janet,

dressed like a pirate's wench, took off running as Rachel chased her across the yard.

Jason watched them go then turned back to Mike who was dressed like Blackbeard the Pirate. "Hey Mike, cool party, huh?"

"You guys run with a pretty wild crowd. I love your costume by the way, who made it?"

"Rachel. She's a woman of many talents." Jason turned and looked over the crowd gathered in Sarah's backyard. "Let's see, three pirates, a serving wench, two hobbits and a wizard, a couple of drag queens, two witches, oh, somebody from Star Wars or maybe Star Trek, I get them confused."

Mike chuckled. "Yeah, I think I saw Princess Leia a moment ago, she had a lip lock on Darth Vader and it looked like his light saber was standing at attention."

Jason shook his head and laughed. "This place is crazy."

Janet returned, dashing behind Mike as Rachel followed her in hot pursuit.

Janet squealed, using Mike as a shield, and then she laughed and threw a towel around Rachel. "Now I'll hug you!" She grabbed Rachel into a big bear hug and, giggling like schoolgirls, they nearly fell to the ground.

Janet collapsed into a lawn chair and Rachel, draping the towel over the chair next to her, did the same.

Rachel grinned. "You run pretty fast for a girl."

"Ha, I ran track in high school." Janet was still panting a bit as she grinned at Rachel. "I finished second in the state championships. But that was a long time ago. I'm out of breath now." Janet glanced over at Jason. "Does that chainsaw work?"

He wiggled his eyebrows like Groucho Marx. "Of course my dear, how do you think Rachel's dress ended up looking the way it does?"

Jason watched Howard walk over to the stereo system under the awning on the patio. He gave the volume knob another twist and the bass reverberated across the yard. "How do the neighbors handle this insanity?"

Janet shouted over all the noise. "They're mostly all here. Sarah looked long and hard to find a place in a neighborhood that was, how should I put this, ah, that was accepting."

"Oh, very cool."

Janet shrugged her shoulders. "Yeah, it is. If I could afford it, I'd have a place around here too."

Rachel stood up and grabbed her towel then she reached over and took Janet's hand. "Come on, I'm thirsty." Both girls walked off in search of the beverage coolers while Jason and Mike took their seats.

"So, how long have you guys been dating?"

Jason set his toy chainsaw on the grass beneath his seat. "We met just before the semester started, so about three months."

"She's gorgeous and she seems like a lot of fun. How did you meet Janet?"

"Here. Sarah invited us over a couple of weeks ago to a backyard barbecue, and before you ask, we met Sarah; actually I met Sarah, a couple of weeks before that. Rachel is an old friend of hers and a big fan of her shoe store. I guess that's how we ended up on the guest list."

Two more pirate wenches ran past them with a

drag queen in hot pursuit welding Howard's super soaker.

"During the barbecue I was sitting near here, trying to keep a low profile, while Rachel caught up with some old friends. Janet sat down in the chair next to me. She didn't know too many people here either so we just started talking. She told us she was open for vacation ideas and wondered if we had any. We started to tell her about our recent trip to Nassau but we got interrupted. The next day she came to my office to hear more about our trip. That's when you saw her."

"It was pure luck that I happened to catch her outside of your office that day. I'm glad I said something to you too, because she called me that weekend. It surprised the hell out of me."

Two more girls ran by waving a pair of men's swimming trunks like they were doing a victory lap at NASCAR. A pant-less Count Dracula followed them in hot pursuit.

"Jason, all I've got to say is, she's amazing. I'm the luckiest guy in the world. We went on our first date last Saturday."

"Where?"

"To dinner and a movie."

"How did it go?"

"I have no idea, I was so nervous I didn't pay attention to anything but her. I was so worried I might do something wrong." He glanced over at Jason with a cock-eyed smile. "I guess it went okay, she asked me over for dinner the following night."

"Great."

"It was, and I think that went well too. At least she hasn't kicked me out yet."

They sat and watched the party for a couple of minutes in silence.

"Jason."

"Yeah."

"Thanks."

"Any time, Mike. I'm glad you and Janet hit it off so well."

"I haven't had this much fun in years."

"They are fun. I guess it's hard for a couple of stuffy academics like us to keep up with them."

Mike stood up with a big grin and struck an exaggerated pose. "Speak for yourself old man, I, on the other hand, am an intellectual and definitely not stuffy." He sat down with a plop and a chuckle.

Janet walked up behind Mike and laughed. "Oh you're stuffed all right." She wrapped her arms around his neck still holding two red solo cups. "But I'm okay with you're stuffing." She nibbled his ear and made him squirm. "Here, I brought my intellectual academic a beer."

Mike grabbed the cup with a silly grin and downed half of it in one gulp. "Thanks honey, you're the best."

Janet walked around Mike and pulled another lawn chair over next to him. "Jason, are we still on for this weekend?"

"The play at the college?"

"Uh-huh."

"Sure, Rachel and I are looking forward to it."

"Cool."

Mike grabbed her hand and gave it a gentle squeeze. "We'll meet you guys in the lobby if that's okay?"

"That works for us."

Janet leaned forward and kissed Mike on the cheek then she glanced at Jason. "And maybe coffee after?"

Rachel walked up with a couple of red solo cups in hand. "Better still, I know this great place that has a fantastic dessert menu for after hours." She handed one of her cups to Jason.

Janet's eyes were sparkling with excitement. "Where's that?"

"It's called The Baker's Oven. They serve a double chocolate brownie smothered in chocolate ice cream and drizzled with chocolate syrup. It is to die for."

Rachel turned the key to open her apartment door. "That was a great party."

"Yes it was."

"Meet you on the terrace in a few? I need to get a shower and wash off all this fake blood."

"Me too, I think half of your blood ended up on me."

"Salsa dancing was fun though, wasn't it?"

Jason reached his hand behind her neck and pulled her lips to his. "You are one hot woman, you know that?"

"Hmm, I love it when you're naughty."

He moved to kiss her again and she placed her finger on his lips. "Not yet sweetie, I need a shower then we can see where this will go."

He kissed her finger and then walked over to her terrace door. "My turn to bring the wine, red or white?"

She paused at the corner of the hallway and looked back at him provocatively. "Red, you're going to need all the stamina you can get tonight." She blew him a kiss and disappeared around the corner leaving him standing with a huge grin.

=TWENTY=

Rachel opened the passenger door of Jason's car and got out. She was wearing a strapless evening dress, low heels, with a matching purse and belt. Jason, wearing a simple suit, moved his hand around her waist as they walked towards the college theatre building.

Waiting near the box office, Mike and Janet waved to them as they entered the lobby. Mike leaned forward and shook Jason's hand. "You guys are running a little late, I was getting worried."

"Sorry Mike. Hi Janet." Jason leaned forward and hugged Janet while Mike shook Rachel's hand. "Have you guys been waiting long?"

Janet chuckled and hugged Mike's arm. "Not really, it gave us time to walk through the Dean's Rose Garden; I just love all the landscaping on this campus."

Mike handed two tickets to Jason. "I picked yours up when I got mine. I think it's almost time, we'd better find our seats."

The four of them found their seats in the middle section of the orchestra level near the back. Rachel looked around at the audience area; this was the first time she had been to a play in years. The last time was in Washington, D.C. Her father took the family there when she was only nine. She remembered that the theatre was decorated in elaborate detail with gilded cornices and columns. This theatre was very plain by comparison. There weren't any gilded columns and the main curtain was pulled back to reveal the stage setting. It looked like a fancy upscale house in the 1940's; the furniture was very stylish and modern but not contemporary.

Rachel glanced down at her playbill. It was a Noel Coward play called *Blithe Spirit.* The director's notes described the play as a ghost story. She leaned over and whispered to Jason. "This is a play about ghosts?"

"Sort of. It's a comedy; one of Coward's most popular. I thought you might like it."

Rachel smiled sweetly and kissed him on the cheek. "You're always thinking of me, aren't you?"

"Always."

The lights slowly dimmed and a diminutive woman entered rather awkwardly and carried a tea tray loaded with china to a coffee table placed downstage of a sofa. The teacups rattled and clanked as she moved with exaggerated care, trying to avoid tipping or, heaven forbid, breaking something.

She started to bend over and place the tray on the coffee table but the teapot began to slide. She stopped a moment and brought the tray back up, jiggling it gently to move the teapot back to the center of the tray. She tried again but the teapot began to slide again. She brought the tea tray back up and glanced around the room frantically.

Suddenly she heard voices coming from off stage. Still faced with the task of placing the tea tray on the coffee table she had only one other choice. She slowly began to spread her legs. Holding the tea tray horizontal, she slowly lowered herself down towards the coffee table. Eventually, her legs splayed out into a full split, and she gently set the tea tray on the coffee table. The audience erupted in applause as the maid wiped her brow and scrambled back to her feet. At that moment a middle-aged couple in evening dress entered through a set of French doors.

The woman paused a moment and looked at the room. "Darling, let's have tea on the verandah, it's so stuffy in here."

The maid looked up and rolled her eyes as the audience roared with laughter.

During the intermission Jason and Mike went to the restroom.

Jason unzipped his pants and leaned in towards the urinal. "You guys doing okay?"

Mike grinned as he zipped up his pants. "Okay? Jason, I simply adore that woman, thank you so much for introducing me to her. She's just wonderful and I hope she feels the same way I do. Did you know she's a massage therapist? She works part-time in a group practice at the Klein building, downtown. She's doing that to put herself through school."

"I'm glad to see you guys hit if off so well."

"Better than well, we're doing great. I owe you big time!"

Jason chuckled and patted Mike on the back as

they exited the restroom.

Out in the lobby Rachel and Janet stood near the theatre entrance waiting for the boys.

"So...what do you think of him?"

"At first it was kind of awkward, but then again, what relationship isn't at first."

"And?"

"Oh Rachel, he's so cute, adorable really. He's not like any other guy I've ever met. He actually listens to me. It's so great between us but I'm waiting for the other shoe to drop."

Sarah reached over and touched Janet's arm. "What? Do you think something bad is going to happen?"

Janet sighed and smiled winsomely. "No, but it's just been my luck with guys. As soon as things start to go well it turns sour and before I know it, it's over."

"Jan it takes two to make this work. I like Mike too, he's funny and charming in an awkward sort of way that's quite endearing."

"I know he's trying hard and so am I. I'm just afraid it'll be like so many times before."

Rachel grabbed Janet's hands and looked her in the eyes. "Stop living in the past, Jan. If you think that way, it's going to happen. Look, I'm the last person to be giving relationship advice but the way I see it, if you want something you have to work for it and not wait for it to come to you."

"I know, I know, thanks. Rachel, you're a good friend, I... Oh, here they come."

After the performance Mike and Janet followed Rachel and Jason over to the late night place she mentioned. The dessert was every bit as decadent as

Rachel promised.

Janet dabbed her mouth with her napkin to wipe away a smudge of chocolate. "You know, I thought that play was going to be a huge bore, but it was great."

Jason nodded. "I need to send a note to my friend Carl in the drama department, his students did a great job."

"Were they all students? I thought some of them looked a bit old to be college students."

"I guess that's the advantage of being in a community college, you get people from all ages."

Rachel grinned as she leaned over and kissed Jason on his cheek. "Well, I thought they did a marvelous job, you can tell your friend Carl I said so."

"Thanks, I will."

The waitress stopped by their table and dropped off the bill. Mike grabbed it up before Jason could get it. "My treat," he grinned as he pulled out his wallet.

Jason smirked and dropped his napkin on his plate. "Then it's my turn next time."

"Deal."

They all stood up and Jason held Rachel's coat for her to slip on. "We probably should get going; I've got a ton of homework waiting for me tomorrow."

After Mike helped Janet with her coat he slipped his arm around her waist. "Me too, no rest for the weary."

Janet hugged Jason and whispered in his ear. "Let's do coffee next week just us girls, okay? I'll call Rachel and set it up."

Jason whispered his reply. "Jessie's still very shy

Janet."

Janet smiled sweetly and sighed. "I know, but maybe just this once?"

Jason glanced at Rachel who nodded back at him with a gleam in her eye. He looked at Janet and shrugged his shoulders.

Janet snuck a tiny peck on his cheek and hugged him again then she hugged Rachel. "I'll call you, okay?"

"Okay."

They continued to whisper as Jason walked over and shook Mike's hand. "See you Monday, Mike."

Mike grinned and glanced over at Janet and Rachel. "What's going on?"

"Girl talk, most likely."

Mike nodded with a knowing smile. "Let's do this again sometime."

"Okay, sounds great."

They stepped out of the cafe door and were greeted with a gentle rain.

Jason shook his head. "Of course, I forgot my umbrella."

Mike grinned. "Me too, see ya." They scrambled for the parking lot to bring their cars around for the girls.

That night Jason and Rachel sat on his couch watching the rain dribble off the awning outside his terrace door. They turned out all the lights, lit several candles, and made gentle passionate love to the rhythm of the falling rain.

She straddled him as he thrust into her, her nails dug into his shoulder as she clenched around his shaft while he moved in and out of her body.

She remembered her aunt Louise telling her once when she was barely sixteen how, if she was willing to look hard and be patient, she would someday find someone who was perfect for her. And Jason was perfect, so beautifully perfect.

She felt him begin to swell; his thrusts were coming faster, stronger, more demanding. She knew he was close. She slammed her body down, squeezing his cock, holding him inside her, possessing him, and never wanting to let him go.

He erupted inside her, coating her vagina with his seed. She hugged him tightly, wrapping her arms around his neck and smothering him with kisses. "Mmm, you make me feel so good...so incredibly good."

Her breathing was still rapid and her body glowed with perspiration. Nearly spent, she collapsed against his chest as he wrapped his arms around her.

They stayed there, listening to the gentle patter of the rain, locked in a lover's embrace. He intoxicated her. The smell of his sweat mixed with the scent of his soap and shampoo. How did she ever get to be so lucky? She guessed her aunt was right...patience brought her someone perfect.

He whispered softly in her ear. "Penny for your thoughts."

"I was thinking about that first day we met. The day I painted your toenails red and slipped my white sandals on your feet."

"I gave you quite a shock that day, didn't I?"

"Uh-huh. You know I still don't know what possessed me to do it, paint your toenails red, I mean. I've never done anything as daring as that before, especially to a complete stranger. I bet you thought I was crazy."

"No, I didn't. I thought you were cute. For that matter, I have no idea why I decided to let you do it, then stand up and walk into my kitchen. I've never done that before either. I've always been so shy about wearing heels in front of anyone, let alone a beautiful woman. It still amazes me."

"I'm glad you did." She felt him soften and begin to slip out of her. She snuggled closer.

They sat quiet for a while, cuddling on his sofa. The rain had slowly tapered off to a fine mist. The air smelled fresh and clean and the streetlights below shimmered with a misty halo. It felt magical.

"What are you thinking about my love?"

"Nassau, that beautiful white gown, and the perfection that is you."

"I love you Jason Davies, with all my heart."

"I love you Rachel Clark, with all my heart too."

=TWENTY=ONE=

"I'm glad you're driving Rachel, this whole thing is so distracting. I know she's going to be pissed. I hate disappointing her, but I just can't be Jessie where people might know me."

"I understand sweetie. I'm sure that Jan will understand too."

"I hope so. I know I went shopping with you before we left for the Bahamas and all, but I felt anonymous in those stores. Not here so close to campus."

Rachel nodded as she pulled into a parking lot of a cozy little dinner on the southside of the community college where Jason and Mike worked. She parked Jason's car near the entrance. They got out and walked through a portico to the front door. The mid-morning breeze was soft, the air was warm and the setting was delightful. Rachel was wearing a cashmere sweater with a shawl, Capri pants, and a pair of three-inch pumps. Jason was dressed casually in slacks, a golf shirt, and a light jacket.

They walked up to hostess. "Hi, we're meeting Janet Tabor."

"Yes sir, right his way, she's waiting for you outside."

They followed her out to the terrace. Janet had selected a table shaded by beautiful old oak trees.

Janet stood up and Rachel wrapped her arms around her. "Hi girl, you look great."

"Thanks, I'm glad you two could join me. Oh. I thought Jessie was coming."

"I'm sorry Jan, I just couldn't."

Janet looked disappointed. "But why?"

Jason sat in a chair next to Rachel. "Jan, even going to Sarah's as Jessie was killing me. I was a nervous wreck the whole time. Besides, I sort of got dragged into that party." He glanced across to Rachel.

She stuck her tongue out with a smirk. "But it was fun wasn't it?"

"Yes, it was fun but I was on pins and needles the whole time. At the same time, Rachel and I wouldn't have met you so that part was actually good. I wish I could make you understand. You can't imagine the fallout if Mike or any of my colleagues, let alone one of my students, ever discovered that part about me."

"I'm one of your students, sort of."

Jason slumped his shoulders and sighed. "Janet…I'm sorry. I just can't."

"I think I understand Jason, I was the same way before I decided to live full-time as a woman. And after that, it was still difficult. It's hard to overcome all the stereotypes let alone the social prejudice."

"But I've never wanted to live as a woman."

Rachel came to Jason's defense. "It was always about the shoes Jan, he loves them. You can't blame him, I love them too."

Janet reached forward and touched Rachel's hand. "We all do!"

Rachel giggled. "Honestly, I've tried to get him into a dress, I think he'd look really cute. But he'll have none of it."

"I'm sorry Jason, I'm not trying to make you feel bad, it's just...I had a such a wonderful time talking to Jessie at Sarah's that, well, I guess I'm a little jealous, I wanted to see her again."

Rachel grabbed Janet's hand. "Hey, I know, why don't you come over to my place next Saturday?" She turned to Jason. "Do you think Jessie will be around?"

"As long as it's just the three of us, I'm sure Jessie would love to join you."

"I'll see if I can get him into one of my skirts." Rachel winked at Janet.

"Not even funny, love."

Both girls giggled and Jason blushed.

"So, how's it going with Mike?"

"I think I'm really falling for him Jason, but I'm nervous. Rachel tells me that everything will be fine if I don't push it. But if I go too slow I'm afraid that he might get tired of me and leave."

"I think you and Mike are really great together. But even in a perfect relationship the devil is in the details. I'm with Rachel on this one. Go slow and savor the moment, don't just jump into bed and expect to ride off into Shangri-La. Sometimes that works, sometimes you hit a few bumps and if you're unprepared to handle them you can end up in a ditch. I know you like him and you want to show him how much you care, but you can find other ways to express yourself."

"Yes, there's nothing wrong with good old fashion necking." Rachel purred as she curled her arm around Jason's, he blushed crimson and smiled shyly.

Janet stood up and drew them into a huge hug. "Thank you guys, you two are the greatest. I can't tell you how much this means to me."

They sat back down as a waiter brought them their desserts.

Rachel's grin grew as she spooned a bite into her mouth. "Hmmm, scrumptious. This place is so quaint, we'll have to come back."

"Jan, Mike told me your a massage therapist, do you have any openings next week?"

Janet opened her purse and pulled out her day planner. "How about Thursday afternoon at two?"

"That works for me, Rachel?"

"Me too, I'll schedule in a medical appointment that afternoon."

"Great, and for you guys it's on the house."

Jason shook his head. "No way, Mike told me you're putting yourself through school. Freebies won't pay tuition."

Rachel nodded. "Yes, and we're heavy tippers too."

A waiter showed up again with coffee and the conversation drifted towards Janet's school plans, her hopes and dreams.

The afternoon slipped towards evening and they parted with promises to meet at Rachel's on Saturday.

=TWENTY-TWO=

Rachel stood in her kitchen, her cellphone cradled on her shoulder, stirring a large pot of soup. "Uh-huh, sure, I'll tell Jason as soon as he comes home."

She heard the familiar thump that announced Jason's arrival.

"Wait, I think he just got home. Hold on I'll go get him." Rachel walked out onto her terrace and stepped over the small dividing wall. She walked over to Jason's sliding door and rapped on the glass.

Jason slid the door open and leaned forward to give her a kiss. "Hi sweetie."

"Jason, my sister's on the phone. She wants to know if we can meet her for coffee tomorrow?"

"Sure, where?"

Rachel put the phone back to her ear. "Where do you want to meet sis?" She paused a moment and then she whispered to Jason. "How about Murray's near Woodhaven?"

Jason nodded and pulled off his coat and tie.

"Okay sis, two o'clock tomorrow. We'll see you then." She walked into Jason's apartment and wrapped her arms around his neck and kissed his cheek. "You know you're going to be under the microscope don't you."

Jason grinned as he hugged her. "It was bound to happen sooner or later."

"I suspect this is all a prelude to inviting us over for Thanksgiving too. Hanna's big on family gatherings. They usually end disastrously but she loves them anyway."

"Great, I haven't been to a big family dinner since I was a kid." He picked her up and twirled her around the room. "Bring on the drama! Is something burning?"

"Oh shit, my soup!

Murray's was a little Ma & Pa diner that survived on good food served quickly with old-fashioned service. Jason and Rachel walked in the front door and were quickly led to a booth near the front of the restaurant. A woman stood with open arms and she reached forward to grab Rachel with glee. They both giggled like schoolgirls.

"Hanna, this is Jason."

Hanna reached out her hand and took Jason's in a firm handshake. "Hello, Rachel has told me all about you and I've been dying to meet you."

"Hi, I'm glad to meet you too."

They sat down in a nearby booth and a waitress handed them their menus. Rachel glanced around and sighed. "Nothing's changed, it like it's frozen in time."

Hanna smiled, following her survey of the

restaurant then laughed out loud. "I know, even some of the waitresses haven't changed either." She looked at Jason. "Daddy used to take us here when we were just girls on Sunday mornings after church. We used to live on Brandon Avenue so it was closer too. He'd tell us that Sunday was Momma's day off too so we'd all pile in the car and head over here for a big brunch." She paused a moment and looked at Jason. "Are you from around here Jason?"

"The world actually, my parents were both in the military. We moved around a lot. Before I left for college I lived in Ohio, near Dayton."

"Do you see your family often?"

"We're not very close and they're both in Europe right now. I see my grandmother from time to time or talk to my cousin. But that's about it for my family. Could you excuse me for a moment? I need to find the restroom. I'll be right back."

Hanna was quite taken by Jason's charm. She told Rachel as much when Jason left.

"That's good because I love him."

"You sound like you're hearing wedding bells."

"Not yet, but maybe."

Hanna sat there for a moment her mouth hanging open in shock. "Has he asked you?"

Rachel blushed crimson and covered the growing smile on her lips. "Nope."

"Oh stop being coy! Tell me!"

"Trust me, my darling sister, you'll be the first to know but there's nothing to tell...yet."

Hanna looked askance. "You sure this isn't puppy love?"

"Sis, it isn't. I've never felt like this about anyone before. He's simply marvelous. He took me flying last month," she squealed.

"What? Where?"

"Kitty Hawk, on the outer banks in North Carolina. It was a promise he made to me when we flew to the Bahamas."

"Wait, what? The Bahamas? You flew? This is coming way too fast."

"Jason suggested we fly to the Bahamas for fall break at his school. He had a four-day weekend. I took some time off from work and we went. Oh Hanna, it was wonderful. We stayed in this dumpy little hotel near the beach but that didn't matter. We were never there anyway. We were either snorkeling, or sailing, or shopping. I loved it!"

"Were you together, I mean in the same room?"

"I'm a big girl Hanna, but no we had separate rooms. We started out just two friends going on a vacation to the Bahamas and we ended up falling in love.

Hanna glanced up but didn't see Jason yet. "You simply must come to Thanksgiving dinner next week. Everyone has to meet Jason. Besides, he took you flying? You mean he flew a plane and you went with him?"

"No, I flew, by myself, in a hang glider. It was crazy fun."

Hanna sat there stunned. "Amazing. Are you even my sister?"

"I know, my life has changed so much. It's been like a magic carpet ride." She sighed blissfully. Then Rachel snapped out of the dream and back into the moment. "So, Thanksgiving. Who all is coming?"

Hanna took a moment to catch up then smiled. "Just Bob and the kids, and Bob's sister Susie, and her husband and two boys. I'm hoping I can pry mom and dad out of Florida for the week as well but I'm not holding my breath."

Rachel fiddled with her menu a moment then looked up. "Is Susie still married to Glenn, the ex-marine?"

"Yes, why?"

She glanced out the window then looked at Hanna, determined. "Because he's such an a-hole, I don't see what she sees in him."

"Rachel, it's the holidays, please come. The family hasn't met Jason yet and he hasn't met the family. I'll ask Bob to speak to Glenn and ask him to cool the conservative rhetoric."

"The right-wing whack-job bombast you mean."

Jason returned from the restroom and slipped back into the booth next to Rachel. "What did I miss?"

"Just girl talk. We're going to Hanna's for Thanksgiving."

"Okay, what can we bring?"

"I love this guy! What other man would think to ask something like that?"

Jason blushed as Rachel kissed him on the cheek then she turned to Hanna. "We'll bring a salad."

Later that afternoon Janet joined them for coffee in Rachel's apartment. She arrived wearing a silky blouse, slacks, and a pair of five inch beige stilettos. Her long hair was pulled back into a bob and she was sporting a fresh coat of pink polish on her nails. When the door opened and she saw Jessie she flew into her arms. "I've missed you Jessie." Then she took in several large breaths and hung off her shoulder. "Oh, wait, I have to catch my breath. You didn't tell me there wasn't an elevator.

"Yeah, sorry about that, it's our daily aerobics, three flights at a time."

Janet nodded and sat down on the couch. "There, that's better."

"I missed you too Janet, I love those shoes. Did you get them at Sarah's?"

She crossed her legs and lifted one foot higher in the air, admiring her shoe. "Yes, they were on sale too. Sorry I'm late; I had to stop by and see my Aunt Jillian. She's going in for eye surgery next week and she's a basket case of worries.

Jessie poured a cup of coffee for Janet and set in on the table for her. "Eye surgery? What's wrong?"

"Cataracts."

Rachel moved over and sat down next to Jessie. "Really? How old is she?"

"Not that old but she teaches metal sculpture at the Art Center. The welding gets to you after a while. I like that blouse Jessie, the color suits you."

"Thanks, I borrowed it from Rachel."

Janet sat quietly for a few minutes. The silence was a bit awkward for everyone. After stirring the cream in her coffee she continued to fiddle with the spoon. It was obvious that something was really bothering her. "Look, I don't know how else to ask this so I guess I'll just blurt it out. I know you two said to go slow and savor the moment but I'm…I don't know, I just want to…you know."

Rachel leaned closer to Janet and squeezed her hand. "I know exactly what you're talking about Jan. I felt the same way about Jason. Too fast, too slow, I nearly went insane trying to decide what to do."

"What did you do?"

"I waited until I found the perfect moment. It wasn't planned, it just happened."

Jason looked a bit shocked at her revelation. "You mean you didn't plan that white dress on the terrace in the Bahamas?"

"No sweetheart." She turned to Janet and smiled. "Sure, I packed the dress, but I didn't know if I was ever going to wear it until I talked with Jason on the beach that night.

"At that moment, standing in the surf, I knew in my heart that the time was right." She leaned over and kissed Jessie on the cheek. "Sometimes you just have to be the one who leads, or at least gives them a gentle push. The difficulty is knowing when and only you will know that."

Jessie sipped her coffee. "Have you said anything to him about this?"

"No...I'm too scared."

"Mike is a lot like Jason, Jan; we've grown up being told by our mothers to not force ourselves on women. So it backfires on them sometimes when girls want us to be more assertive. Mixed signals are hard to read.

Rachel leaned forward and winked at Jessie, and then she turned to Janet. "Turn up the heat a little, you have a beautiful body Jan, use it. If Jessie's right and Mike is anything like Jason, put on five-inch stilettos and a plunging neckline and he'll be putty in your hands."

Jessie nodded. "So true."

Rachel got up and walked into the kitchen to pour herself another cup of coffee. "I know, give him a special treat for Thanksgiving. He'll never forget that holiday, I guarantee it."

"Speaking of Thanksgiving, Rachel and I just got invited to her sister's for the big meal."

"Do you have a big family Rachel?"

"No, it was just me and my sister. My parents moved to Florida when I went to college and my sister lives north of the city in the suburbs. She's married with two kids."

"How about you Jessie?"

"My family are all military so they're on the move all the time. I'm not very close to any of them except my cousin Karen and my grandmother; both of them live in Cleveland. How about you?"

"I'm from the typical suburban family, husband, wife, three kids, a dog and a cat. We grew up in New Jersey near Trenton. Mom and Dad are still there, retired now. I was the baby of the family. Mom thought they were stopping at two until I came along." She grinned sheepishly. "I was conceived in the backseat of a 59 Chevy. My dad is an old car buff."

"Growing up in the 'burbs' meant the usual things, cub scouts, baseball, soccer. Because I was the youngest I probably had it the easiest. My older brother was the trailblazer in the family. He was the one who Dad was the hardest on. Which is probably why Tom was so angry when I decided to go through the change. I think he'd always been a bit jealous of the way Dad was with me. Beth, my sister, was indifferent. As long as I didn't try to be a part of her life, she didn't care one way or the other. Of course that meant I couldn't see my nieces either, or Tom's twins."

Her eyes began to tear up. Rachel handed her a

tissue and she dabbed them dry. "Thanks."

Jessie stood up and walked over to Janet. She sat down next to her and wrapped her arm around her shoulder. She relaxed a little and smiled meekly.

"So, I moved here and started over. That was three years ago. I didn't start living full-time as a woman until I had some work done. These," she lifted her breasts slightly, "and a little nip and tuck up here," her hand brushed by her cheeks and throat, "needed to be done to complete the look."

Rachel leaned forward and took her hand. "They did beautiful work Jan, you're gorgeous."

Janet blushed and sent Rachel an air-kiss. "Flatterer."

"Anyway, jobs were difficult until after the surgery. I finally landed the design assistant job downtown last year. It's hard work and the hours can be long sometimes, but fun, well," she chuckled, "sometimes it's fun."

Jessie stood up and got a cup of coffee from the counter. She turned and sat on a stool. "When did you meet Brie?"

"Oh, at work actually. She was an assistant to one of the firm's clients. We hit it off but not sexually. She was into hunks like the two doorknobs she introduced me too at Sarah's when I met you guys. Don't get me wrong, I like Brie, but her fascination with six-pack abs is so boring."

Rachel smiled and nodded. "Your family, are they supportive? Other than your brother and sister, I mean."

"No. I'd been sneaking HRT drugs for a couple of years before my mom found out. A friend of mine introduced me to a pharmacist in North Philly who helped me…for a price, of course. That went along fine for a while. My body was beginning to change, to soften and get curvy. I even had breasts; they were smaller then but natural. Everything was fine until I broke my arm."

"What happened?"

"Skateboarding. Mom took me to the doctor and he did some routine blood tests. When the results came back Mom and Dad exploded. When the dust settled six months later I was on a bus coming here and looking for work."

Everyone was quiet for a moment then Jessie smiled and nodded. "Rachel is right, Thanksgiving is just perfect."

Janet looked up quizzically.

"Mike is by himself. His family lives in Muncie, Indiana. In the past he usually called up a coupe of his friends to hang out and watch football. He was going to invite me too, but when I started dating Rachel that all changed. This is great. Call him, right now. Invite him over for an early dinner."

Janet glanced at Rachel. "Should I? Now?"

"If you want we can go out onto the terrace while you call him."

"No, no, please stay." She rummaged through her purse and pulled out her cellphone, quickly dialed, and then listened to it ring.

"Hi Mike, it's me Janet. Uh-huh, do you have plans for Thanksgiving? Uh-huh. Would you like to join me for an early dinner? Great! Around four o'clock maybe? Cool. What can you bring? I don't know, ah…"

Janet glanced over to see Jessie frantically waving his hands. He mouthed the word 'dessert'.

"How about you bring the dessert? Great. Yes? Oh, no problem, say hi to Jason when you see him next week. Yeah, bye." She collapsed on the sofa in giggles and smiles.

Janet lifted her hand and held her finger close to her thumb. "Now there is only one more teensy little issue."

Rachel and Jessie leaned forward. "What?"

"I don't know how to cook."

=TWENTY-THREE=

Jessie leaned back and smiled. "No problem, we'll help."

Rachel took another sip of her coffee. "We can go shopping with you next Tuesday. We can pick up the bird and all the fixings. Then we'll help you prep everything. All you will have to do is turn on the oven and pop the bird in at the right time. Piece of cake!"

"Why Tuesday?"

"So that the turkey has time to thaw."

"Oh."

The next few days flew by and Janet met Rachel and Jason at the local grocery store on the Tuesday before Thanksgiving. They were there to buy everything on her shopping list for Thursday's big event.

Jason pushed a shopping cart down the canned goods aisle looking for bargains. "We'll help you with all the prep early Thursday morning. Which means

185

we'll be at your place by 7am."

Janet looked aghast. "In the morning?"

"Yup. Here, pick up a couple of those cans of sweet yams."

"Seven in the morning?"

"Yes, dear, seven. You need time to prep the bird before it goes in the oven and that will have to happen by nine or the turkey won't be ready for an early afternoon dinner."

"My mom used to get up at five because she usually cooked a big bird." Rachel turned and started to dash off towards the produce section. "Oh, I almost forgot. We need some fresh cranberries. Nothing says Thanksgiving like fresh cranberries set on the dinner table."

Jason laughed as Rachel disappeared around the corner. "Next to sweet yams smothered in golden marshmallows."

Janet's eyes began to sparkle. "Yum."

They continued down the aisle picking up a few more can goods along the way. A moment later Rachel joined them tossing several bags of fresh cranberries in the basket. "Come on, the turkey's are in the freezer section around the corner up ahead."

Janet was beginning to look a little overwhelmed. "How big of a bird should I buy?"

Rachel tossed in a can of green beans as they passed that section on their way to the freezer area. "Well, if it's just going to be the two of you I'd go for a small one."

Jason pushed the cart to the end of the aisle. "But if she gets a bigger one she'll have left overs into next week."

"That's true. What do you think Jan?"

"I think I'll split the difference."

Before long they had finished their shopping and they started loading groceries into Jason's car. "We'll take the groceries to your place where you can set the turkey out to thaw on Wednesday."

Janet wrapped her arms around Rachel and Jason and gave them both a big hug. "I don't know how to thank you guys for all of this."

Jason's stomach began to rumble. "Come on, all this food shopping has made me hungry. Let's stop somewhere for a bite to eat."

It was Thursday morning and Janet stumbled out of her bedroom to a persistent knocking on her front door. "I'm coming."

"Morning sunshine."

Janet stood in the doorway wiping the sleep from her eyes. "Ugh, what time is it?"

Rachel dropped her purse on the couch near the kitchen and turned to look in the refrigerator. "It's time to put on your apron and become the master chef that you're destined to be."

In no time the three of them were working diligently in Janet's kitchen. Rachel looked skeptically at the oven. "Does this thing even work, Jan?" She attempted to adjust the oven temperature and the knob fell off.

Janet reached down and replaced the broken knob. "I think so, all I ever do is reheat pizza and occasionally I make soup on the stovetop. I've been meaning to speak to the landlord about it. I guess now is not a good time, huh?"

"Well, we don't have any choice so let's hope for the best. Here," she pointed Janet towards the cranberries, "rinse these off in cold water a couple of times. Jason you can start with the yams since that's your specialty."

Jason nodded and everyone set about their tasks. In a matter of minutes Janet's kitchen was transformed under Rachel's leadership. By nine o'clock, the turkey was prepped, stuffing was mixed, and the vegetables were ready to go into the oven at the appropriate time.

Rachel finished making a note for Janet. "Here, I've made a checklist for you. Just follow the time schedule and you'll do great. You'll have to do some shuffling around in the oven to make everything fit but it should be large enough to work." She picked up her coat and began to put it on. "If you have any questions just give us a call. We'll be at my sisters for most of the afternoon but I know you'll be fine."

"You guys!" Janet hugged them both.

Jason picked up his coat and put it on. "Oh, don't forget to use some cooking spray in the pan for the dinner rolls. They're nearly impossible to get out without it."

Janet nodded and waved.

Rachel grabbed her purse and blew Janet a goodbye kiss on their way out her front door.

Downstairs she slipped into the passenger seat as Jason closed her door. He walked around his car and sat behind the wheel. "That was fun."

"Yeah, it was. We're like an old married couple sending our daughter off to make a dinner for her new boyfriend, aren't we?"

Jason chuckled as he started his car. "We make a good team."

"Yes we do." She leaned over and wrapped her

arms around his neck. She kissed him tenderly on the lips then stayed there a moment gazing into his eyes. Jason closed his eyes and pulled her close, the scent of her shampoo and perfume was intoxicating.

She reached down to his crotch and felt him swell under her touch.

He smiled. "I am putty in your hands, aren't I my love?"

Rachel moved her hand up to caress his cheek. "Just like I am in yours, darling."

Jason took a big breath and let it out with a sigh. "I suppose if we don't get going, we're not going to make it to your sisters' with that salad we promised."

"Rain check in bed tonight sweetheart?"

Jason nodded and kissed her on the lips. "Happy Thanksgiving, my love."

Rachel sighed contentedly. "Happy Thanksgiving."

=TWENTY-FOUR=

Janet stepped out of the shower and toweled off her hair. She wiped the fog off the mirror and examined her breasts. The marks from the surgery were nearly invisible now. It seemed like it took forever to heal but it was well worth it. They stood out proudly with beautiful areolas and nipples perched like little plums still aroused from the pelting hot water of the shower. She pinched them a moment and imagined what Mike's caress might be like, so soft and tender yet passionate and adoring. She moved her hand to her penis and felt it stiffen under her caress.

She wondered what his touch would be like. Would he take her in his mouth? She began to stroke her cock as it continued to grow. She was aware that her penis was getting a little smaller, a side effect of the hormones she was flooding into her body since she started the therapy several years ago. The doctors warned her that it would probably happen. It was a risk she was willing to take; to have the body her mind told her she should have. She thought about the final surgery, "the big cut" they called it. It made her nervous to consider it but she knew that she had to face that decision some day. Perhaps Mike would be there to help her. The thought made her heart beat faster and her face flush. Was she falling in love? Could it happen so soon? Did he feel the same way?

She shook her head to free her hair from the confines of a towel then she moved her hands to take another towel and dry off her waist and hips. They were rounder now, more supple and soft. She was finally getting to look more feminine. She imagined Mike's hands on her hips, gently brushing against her, teasing her with his caresses. It made her breath catch. She wanted him. Did he want her? What would he think when he finally saw her naked?

She heard a beeper go off in her kitchen. It was nearly ten o'clock now. Rachel told her to check the bird every hour to make sure things were progressing on schedule. She pulled her robe off the hook on the bathroom door and wrapped it tightly around her.

As she padded into the kitchen she noticed that she didn't smell anything, not a whiff. Something was wrong. She felt the stove. It was stone cold. "Fuck." She opened the oven door and felt inside. Nothing, nada, it was as cold as when she put it in there an hour ago. "Fuck, fuck, fuck."

She picked up her cellphone and quickly dialed Rachel. A moment later Rachel answered. "Hi Jan, what's up?"

"My stove quit."

"What? Just now?"

"Yeah. The bird is as cold as when I put it in there. What should I do?"

"Bring it over to my place. You can use my stove."

"Everything?"

"You haven't got any choice, Jan. Jason and I have already left for my sisters. There's a spare key under the doormat."

"Thanks Rachel, you're a lifesaver. I'll be over in a half-hour."

"Call me if you need anything else. I'm sorry I can't be there for you but we're running late."

Janet chuckled. "No problem, I'll figure it out. Go have fun at your sisters. I'll talk to you later after this disaster is averted."

Janet dashed back into her bedroom and threw on a pair of jeans, a t-shirt, and a sweater. Then she pulled out the dress she planned on wearing for Mike after she finished cooking dinner. She hung it on a hook near her dresser and pulled on a pair of shoes. Then she grabbed her purse and headed for the kitchen.

After she loaded all the pans filled with cranberries, yams, and vegetables into her car she pulled the turkey out of her stone-cold oven and walked out of her apartment. As she heard her front door click shut she realized that her purse was still sitting on the kitchen counter, her keys were laying next to it. She must have laid them there inadvertently during one of her trips from her apartment to her car. She stood there and shook her head slowly. "Fuck, shit, damn."

She carried the turkey down to her car and loaded it into the back seat. Then she reached under the dashboard and pulled out a magnetic key holder she placed there for just such an occasion. This wasn't the first time she'd locked herself out of her apartment. Luckily, her car was unlocked this time.

She dashed back upstairs and grabbed her purse and keys. Then she locked her front door again and headed back down to her car in the parking lot. Twenty minutes later and only two blocks from Rachel's apartment, her luck ran out again. BAM! The rear tire on the driver's side just blew out. And it was the spare.

"Damn it all to hell!" She leaned against the steering wheel and started to cry. She wiped her eyes and opened her door.

Standing next to the car she looked at the flat tire with disgust. Her shoulders slumped as she leaned against the driver's side door. She knew that she couldn't ask Rachel or Jason for help, they were probably already at her sisters. They'd already done so much.

Her friend Brie was no use; she was out of town visiting her sister in Detroit. Her only other choice was to call Mike. She didn't want to, she wanted to come off looking all together like the heroine always looks in the movies. But life just wasn't going to let her get away with that today. She pulled out her cellphone and called him.

Mike answered on the third ring. "Hey babe, how's it going? I'm getting hungry just thinking about what you're cooking."

"Hi Mike, yeah, about that."

"What's wrong?"

"I have a flat tire and it's my spare."

"Really? Where are you?"

"26th and Grove near Rachel and Jason's apartment building."

"What are you doing over there?"

"It's a long story sweetheart, can you come help me fix it?"

"I'm on my way." Rachel could hear Mike's door slam shut in the background. "Do you have a jack and tire iron in you car?"

"Yup, just no spare tire."

"Okay, I'll be there in a jiffy, bye."

Janet glanced at her car and noticed all the food sitting on her backseat. She decided to cover it up so hopefully he wouldn't see it. She didn't want to look foolish even though she felt like it. She set her jaw as she crossed her arms with a huff. On Monday she was going to get a new set of tires for her car and call that stupid landlord to fix her stove.

Twenty minutes later Mike pulled up next to her. The grin on his face went from ear to ear as he stepped from his car.

Janet blushed as she turned away from his broad grin. "Well, you don't have to be so cheerful about it."

"Ah, come on, sweetie, I get to be the hero who rides in on the white horse. Well, white Honda actually." Mike gathered her up in his arms and kissed her cheek.

She looked back into his eyes and smiled demurely. "Thank you." She leaned forward and kissed him gently on the lips.

"Now, let me help you get that tire off." He started to walk around to her trunk when he glanced into the back seat of her car. "Hey, what do you have in there?"

She sighed. She was found out. "Dinner."

"What?"

"It was going to be our dinner today but my stove broke so I was going over to Rachel's to use her stove."

"And then bring it all back to your place before I arrived? You're amazing."

"Amazingly bad luck is what I have today."

"Well today, your bad luck is my good fortune."

"What do you mean?"

"When you invited me over for dinner today I wanted to help. But you sounded like you had it all together and didn't need me. So I've been sitting around all morning wishing I was with you and now here I am."

Tears began to trickle down her cheeks. "I wanted to make a good impression, I wanted you to think that," she wiped the tears from her cheeks. "That I could be somebody you wanted to keep in your life."

"Oh babe, I decided that the first time I saw that cute butt of yours sashay down the hallway outside of Jason's office. Every day I'm with you I learn so much more about you." He pulled her back into his arms. "I adore you Janet Tabor and you're definitely someone I want to keep in my life." He leaned forward and kissed her on the lips then he lingered there as she kissed him back.

"Now come on, let's move the food into my car. We can cook it at my place. The kitchen's small but everything works, at least it did the last time I checked."

She swatted his arm playfully. "Not even funny."

=TWENTY-FIVE=

In the family room next to the kitchen Jason sat with Hanna's husband, Bob and his brother-in-law Glenn watching a pro-football game on the television. The half-time commentary started and the commentators are talking about a faux pas of ESPN reporters who, in the past, seemed to take an unusual interest in the new player, Michael Sam, and his showering habits.

The first commentator chuckled. "It might be interesting to note that the reporter didn't mention anything about any of the other players and their showering habits."

The second commentator added. "According to the Washington Post, ESPN, who proudly bills itself as "The Worldwide Leader in Sports," regretted becoming the worldwide leader in unnecessary, awkward reports on the showering habits of Michael Sam, the first openly gay player drafted into the NFL."

The first commentator chimed in. "Even though

he was cut from the Ram's roster later on, but they claim that action was in no way connected to his sexual orientation."

"Right after the incident, ESPN went on to say that their reporter, Josina Anderson, discussed Sam's showering habits when asked how he was fitting in with teammates during an episode of "Sports Center." In a brief statement issued by ESPN PR staffers shortly after her report, the sports media giant expressed regret for the segment."

"The Washington Post, in a follow up, went on to say, "As the world waits to see whether Michael Sam will survive the St. Louis Rams' first round of cuts Tuesday, ESPN's Josina Anderson delivered a report from Rams headquarters about his shower etiquette. We learned from Ms. Anderson that "another Rams defensive player told me that "Sam is respecting our space" and that, from his perspective, he seems to think that Michael Sam is kind of waiting to take a shower, so as not to make his teammates feel uncomfortable. A little later in the day, Chris Long had a message for the sports network on Twitter: "Everyone but you is over it.""

The first commentator chuckled. "Well, eventually it didn't matter, since he was cut."

The second commentator joined in the laughter. "But it did get the ESPN switch board to light up!"

Glenn slammed down the sporting section of the newspaper and glared at the television. "Fucking faggots! We don't need guys like that in the NFL, I'm glad they cut the little queer. We need real men cracking heads not faggot boys having tea parties."

Jason rolled his eyes. Glenn was making more noise than sense as he shouted at the television and

Bob.   Hanna's husband didn't seem to be bothered by any of it. Jason stood up and walked towards the kitchen.

Bob chortled as he flipped the channel to another game. "He wasn't little, Glenn, he was well over two hundred pounds dripping wet."

"Ha, ha. Dripping wet, that's funny!"

Near the kitchen doorway Jason struck a rather Shakespearean pose. "Me thinks he doth protest too much."

Glenn spun around in his chair.   "What is he saying?"

Jason turned around with a grin. "Poor hearing from sporadic gun fire, Glenn?" He turned back and walked into the kitchen.

"Turn the TV down Bob." The volume on the television lowered a bit as Glenn stood up and walked to the kitchen door. "Now what was that smart-assed comment you just said?"

"Actually it was Shakespeare who said it, I just repeated it. It's been my experience, and probably his too, that those who protest too much about anything are secretly attracted to whatever it is that they outwardly distain while using bombast as a screen to mask their true intentions."

"Speak in English, boy, this is America! Are you saying I'm queer?!"

"Not a bit Glenn, but I wonder if deep down inside you might be a teensy bit curious."

Glenn launched himself across the kitchen swinging both fists at Jason. "I'll fucking kill you, you faggot lover!"

Jason ducked and slipped past Glenn's ape-like advance and moved quickly to the opposite side of the island counter.

Hanna screamed at him. "Glenn, stop it! Glenn, you're going to hurt somebody."

Glenn slammed into a cabinet sending glassware crashing to the floor.

"AH! My crystal!"

Rachel scoffed. "From the looks of it, it will probably be him!"

Hanna screamed again. "Rachel, you're not helping! Damn it Glenn, get out of my kitchen!" Hanna grabbed a broom and dustpan. "Bob! Come in here and fix this!"

Glenn pulled a frying pan off the rack suspended over the island counter and swung wildly at Jason.

Jason grabbed the broom out of Hanna's hands and parried Glenn's frying pan attacks like a swashbuckling Errol Flynn. He continued to dodge and weave around Glenn's awkward advances. They seemed to be coming more from rage than skill or training.

Jason started chanting with a Spanish accent as he waved the broom handle above his head. He was quoting a line from one of his favorite movies, *Princess Bride*. "My name is Inigo Montoya. You killed my father. Prepare to die."

Hanna shouted at Rachel. "Stand back sis, you're going to get hit by this maniac."

Rachel ducked under the swing of a frying pan. "Which maniac are you talking about?"

"Bob get in here!"

"Rachel, you need to get out of the kitchen. Jason, give me my broom back! Bob!"

Rachel raced around the island counter as Jason's broom handle swept across the room to connect with

Glenn's frying pan. "Yeah, she's probably right. Jason, do you want to go?" The broom handle locked under the frying pan and Jason twisted his wrist to send the pan flying across the room to smash against the side of Hanna's glassware cabinet."

Hanna screamed. "Ah, watch out for my china! That's enough, both of you!"

Bob stormed into the kitchen to stand in front of Glenn. "Come on Glenn, the second half is starting." Glenn made several more feeble attempts to get around Bob then gave up and walked back into the den.

Jason stood anxiously on the opposite side of the counter as Glenn followed Bob back into the living room. They crunched across broken glass and china strewn across Hanna's kitchen floor.

Jason took the dustpan from Hanna with a shrug. "I'm ready whenever you are Rachel." He began to sweep up the broken pieces of stemware on the floor. He stood up and deposited the shards of glass in the trashcan. "Thank you for a lovely meal Hanna, it was nice to meet Bob and your children too."

Hanna sighed as she assessed the damage to her cabinet. "I'm so sorry Jason, Glenn can be such a prick sometimes."

Rachel snorted her disgust.

Hanna smiled meekly then wrapped her arms around Rachel to give her a big hug. "I'm sorry sis, I guess we can't have a family holiday without some sort of disaster."

Rachel shrugged and hugged her back. "It's a family tradition."

"Why don't you guys come over for a Christmas brunch? It'll be just us this time."

Rachel gave her sister a hug and a kiss on the cheek. "Maybe, we'll see what we're doing, okay?"

"Call me."

Rachel nodded to her. Then she followed Jason out the side door to the driveway.

They walked slowly down the driveway towards Jason's car, hand in hand.

"Where did you learn to handle a broom like that?"

Jason shrugged his shoulders and wrapped his arm around hers. "I took stage combat classes in college before I was in *The Pirates of Penzance*."

"You're kidding."

Jason struck a pose in the middle of her sister's driveway. "I am the very model of a modern Major General, I've information vegetable, animal, and mineral. I know the kings of England and I quote the fights historical, from Marathon to Waterloo, in order categorical. I'm very well acquainted, too, with matters mathematical. I understand equations, both simple and quadratical. In short, in matters vegetable, and animal, and mineral I am the very model of the modern Major General."

"Ha!" Rachel squealed with delight. "That was fantastic."

He bowed sweeping his arms wide. "Thank you my dear, performances are sporadic but I always play to a packed house."

Rachel clapped her hands then she smiled meekly. "Do you want to come here for Christmas?"

"Do you?"

She shrugged then she wrapped her arm around Jason's and leaned up to kiss his cheek. "Kind of, I know it's a bit much to ask after everything that happened today but, she is my sister and she's always been there for me. We don't have to stay long."

"Okay. On one condition, I get you all to myself on Christmas morning."

"Thank you, sweetheart."

Suddenly, Rachel's cellphone began to ring. She pulled it out of her purse. "It's Janet."

Jason could hear Janet giggle into the receiver. "We're at Mikes place. Come over, there's plenty of food."

Rachel followed Jason to his car. "What are you doing there?"

"Come over and I'll explain."

Forty-five minutes later Jason and Rachel arrived at Mike's home and over a glass of wine Janet laid out the whole crazy story. "And that's how the turkey trotted all the way over here."

Jason lifted his glass of wine to clink it against the other three. "Well, this is one Thanksgiving that none of us will soon forget."

Mike looked from Jason to Rachel. "Why? What happened to you guys?"

Jason explained the whole event, blow by blow, from Glenn spouting off about gays in the NFL to attacking him in the kitchen with a frying pan.

Janet just sat there and shook her head. The look on her face spoke volumes.

Rachel snorted as she swatted Jason's arm playfully. "Well it didn't help when you started quoting Shakespeare, which was like waving a red flag in front of that bull."

Jason laughed out loud. "Bull is right. He must have broken half a dozen glasses with that frying pan.

Hanna was furious. I'm surprised she didn't thump him herself."

Janet smiled as she stood up and carried several plates back into Mike's kitchen. "Did you guys get enough to eat? There's plenty more where that came from."

Jason patted his tummy. "I'm fine. Rachel?"

Rachel stood up and followed Janet into the kitchen. "I'm good Jan, let me help you with the dishes."

Janet filled the sink with soapy water while Rachel picked up a dishtowel to dry. "So, how was dinner?"

Janet blushed crimson and smiled demurely. "He's just so wonderful. I was having a really crappy day, and he just came in, swooped me into his arms, and I melted."

"Have you?" Rachel's voice tapered off to a whisper. "You know, what we talked about?"

Janet shook her head while smiling impishly. "Maybe tonight," she giggled and then covered her mouth with her fingers. "Don't you dare say a word."

"My lips are sealed and good luck."

An hour later the sun was beginning to settle between the trees. It was beckoning another crisp fall night. Jason stood up and held out his hand for Rachel. "We should probably go, sweetheart. I have tons of shopping to do tomorrow morning and I want to get it done early if I can."

Mike scoffed as he stood up and cleared the rest of the dessert dishes. "You're crazy if you're going shopping tomorrow morning. It's a total zoo out there."

Jason helped Rachel with her coat. "Have you

ever done it?"

"What, go shopping on 'Black Friday'? Never. I've watched the news coverage of people acting like an angry mob too many times to believe that I could ever want to be any part of it."

"That's kind of why I go, to watch the insanity. I get a front row seat."

"How?"

"Mostly I stand in the back with my camera. I have a whole catalogue of crazy things that people have done to try to be first in line. Just to save ten bucks off the price of a toaster! It's insane."

"I know!"

Jason turned as he zipped up his coat. "I've even thought of doing a journal article on it." His eyes sparkled with mischief. "Come with me."

"What?"

"Come with me. I'll pick you up tomorrow at five in the morning. Our first stop after coffee will be the Wal-Mart on Lincoln Street."

"You're crazy! Five a.m.?"

Jason's grin grew wider. "Sure, we'll let the girls sleep in while we look for their Christmas presents."

Mike paused a moment and glanced at Janet. "He's nuts isn't he?" She shrugged her shoulders. Then he glanced at Rachel, and then to Jason. "Okay, you're on. Five it is. But you owe me for waking me at such an un-godly hour."

"No problem. How about we do dinner at my place Christmas evening? It'll be just the four of us. We're going to Rachel's sisters' place for lunch but after that it can be just us. How's that sound?"

Mike looked at Janet who nodded enthusiastically. "Deal."

As Mike ushered Jason and Rachel out his front door. He turned to see Janet leaning on the balcony rail outside of his living room.

Janet felt him wrap his arms around her waist and nuzzled her neck. "That was a spectacular dinner, you really outdid yourself."

She relished his attention. She turned and wrapped her arms around his neck. "You know I'm not a cook don't you?"

"You're just a late bloomer that's all. How about we collaborate again this weekend? I think I would really enjoy working with you in my kitchen on a regular basis."

"You would, would you?"

"Uh-huh." Mike leaned in to her and kissed her gently on the lips. As the kiss became more passionate he lowered a hand to squeeze her butt.

She moaned softly and pressed her body closer to his. "That was lovely."

"Yeah, it was."

"Mike, you do know about me don't you?"

He nodded and leaned in to kiss her again. "Yes. I also know that you've had a difficult time with guys in the past. But I'm not one of those guys." He leaned in and kissed her again. "Janet, I really like you and I really want us to be more than just friends."

"I want that too, but I'm scared." She hugged him tightly. "I don't want to screw this up."

"I'm scared too. Scared that I will do something to chase you away, or hurt you, or something stupid."

"You won't, I'm tougher than I look." She leaned back and looked into his eyes. "Would you make love to me?"

"Yes. How could I deny the most beautiful girl in the world?"

Janet blushed as she hugged him tightly again. Then she released him and took his hand as he led her back through the atrium doors.

Mike led her through the bedroom door to stop at the foot of his bed. He looked into her eyes and blushed. "I'm sorry the room is such a mess, I guess I'm not much of a housekeeper."

She began to slowly unbutton his shirt. "I'm not looking at your room dear, just you."

He reached forward and to do the same but she giggled and stopped him. "Let's take turns. I'll do your shirt first then it's your turn."

She continued to unbutton his shirt, pulling it off his shoulders and letting it fall to the floor. It was his turn next and he unbuttoned the back of her dress and slipped it off her shoulders. The silk fabric bellowed gently and fell in soft folds around her ankles. She smiled shyly, standing in her lingerie as she reached forward to unfasten his belt and let his trousers fall to the floor.

As he removed her bra her natural breasts swung free. Her nipples were standing tall like little ripe fruit waiting for his tongue. He leaned forward and took one nipple in his mouth while caressing the other with his fingers and thumb.

Janet swooned under his touch, her heartbeat grew rapid and the cock in her panties ached to be released. She wanted this; she wanted him to touch her, to caress her. She yearned for the release that she knew was waiting for her. She moved her hands down his sides and hooked her thumbs inside the waistband of his boxers. She slowly drew them down and let them crumple to the floor on top of his trousers. She looked up into his eyes as she let her lips caress the tip of his cock.

He closed his eyes and filled his hands with the locks of her hair as he encouraged her to take him into her mouth, to go deeper, to fill her mouth with his cock.

She began to suck and lick his cock starting on the underside and moving to the tip before plunging him into her mouth. She moved up and down his shaft, drawing him into her, sucking him hard. She could feel ever vein and muscle, every throb of his heartbeat as he moved past her lips. Then she felt him lift her up from the floor.

"You're so incredibly beautiful Jan." He leaned in and kissed her gently on the lips then he knelt down and pulled her satin panties off. "I want to see you, all of you." He let them drop to the floor as he stood up and then he stepped back to admire her. "You are stunning. I had no idea how beautiful you are."

She blushed crimson standing there feeling vulnerable. He stepped forward and took both of her hands to pull her towards his bed. He fell backwards and she fell on top of him, giggling nervously but gleefully. "Make love to me Michael, slow, sweet, and delicious love."

He nuzzled her neck and murmured, "Yes."

"Do you have any…?"

"Top drawer, beneath the condoms," he whispered.

She sat up and straddled him as she reached over to open the nightstand drawer. She pulled out a bottle of lubricant and a condom, which she opened and rolled onto his throbbing cock. She opened the lubricant and applied a liberal dose on his cock. "It's been a while, I might be a little tight."

Mike smiled and shrugged his shoulders. "It's been a while for me too but I'll be as gentle as I can. Just let me know if you want to wait or stop. It's okay, we have plenty of time."

She coated his condom-covered cock and reached behind to push some lubricant past her rosebud. The feeling sent shivers up her spine. He wanted her. He wanted her as much as she wanted him. He called her stunning. No one has ever called her stunning before. She nearly melted as he pressed his cock against her opening.

She pulled her butt cheeks apart and helped him ease past her sphincter. Another gentle thrust and he was inside. It felt so good, so wonderfully good to feel so full. She leaned down and wrapped her arms around his neck pulling him close and smothering him with kisses. "Oh God, you feel so good inside me. Go slow darling, let me catch up, you feel so big."

He slowed down and waited for her. She could feel him throbbing inside. She was slowly getting used to having a cock inside her again. It felt so good. It was different than with her ex-boyfriend, all he wanted to do was slam into her. Like she was some sort of blow-up fuck toy. He didn't give a shit about her; he didn't give a shit about anything except the little appendage that swung between his legs.

Mike was different, way different. She could feel how he felt about her in the way he made love to her, the way he held her, caressed her, kissed her, and even gazed into her eyes.

As she lowered herself down his shaft once again she looked into his eyes. She felt a connection. Was it love? Was this what it really felt like? It was nothing like she had ever felt for any other before, ever. She felt him swell inside her. He was close. She moved her hand to stroke her own hard cock. She wanted to come with him, together, in a single moment of bliss.

He arched his back and she arched hers. She stroked her cock furiously. She felt her come flow as she felt his cock thrust hard inside her. As she felt his seed fill the condom inside her, long ropes of her own cum splashed across his chest and stomach. She collapsed onto his chest, rubbing her cum between them. It felt heavenly.

=TWENTY-SIX=

Mike opened the passenger door and climbed into the seat next to Jason. "Hey, it's cold this morning." He could see his breath in the morning air.

"Yeah, coffee?"

"Absolutely, there's a coffee shop open early around the corner."

Jason started the car and roared off in the direction that Mike pointed. "Perfect."

Twenty minutes later they pulled into the Wal-Mart parking lot. Jason stopped the car further out than usual. "I like to park out here so that I don't find myself in the fray once the fists start flying."

"It gets that crazy?"

"Sometimes, especially if it's early and some of the guys have been camped out here since dusk."

"What do we do now?"

"Finish our coffee and wait until 6am then all hell will break loose."

Mike shook his head as he sipped his coffee.

"Thanks again for helping out Janet yesterday. She tried so hard to make a perfect meal and in spite of all that happened she pulled it off beautifully. Of course I have to thank Rachel for such a detailed list. That girl is a wonder."

"Yes, she is."

"You guys getting serious?"

Jason nodded then he glanced at Mike with a wink. "Yeah, I think we've almost decided that we can't live without each other. I know it's only been about four months but somehow it just seems like it was meant to be. You know?"

Mike nodded his head and took another sip of coffee.

"What about you and Janet?"

"I feel the same way, but we've only known each other for a couple of months, and we don't live next door to one another like you and Rachel do."

"True, it seems like from the very start we were inseparable."

"Jan and I have separate lives but at the same time I'm thinking of her constantly. Yesterday was killing me until she called. I wanted to be there and help her."

"Well, as it turned out you were exactly where you needed to be."

"Yeah, funny how things work out like that."

Jason set his coffee down and picked up his camera. He took off the lens cap and swept across the parking lot looking through his telephoto lens. "So, have you guys gotten together yet?"

Mike grinned from ear to ear. "Yup."

"And?"

"And that's all you're going to get buddy. I don't

kiss and tell. But I will tell you that it was the most remarkable night I have ever had. She is incredible."

Jason smiled then glanced back into the viewfinder. "Uh-oh, it looks like the natives are restless."

"Time to go?"

"Yeah, grab that spare camera and shoot from another angle. This ought to be fun. They have lots of electronics on sale so the fights should be spectacular. I can see the hits on YouTube even now."

They both got out of Jason's car and dashed towards the front doors of the store wearing silly grins.

As they got closer the noise from the crowd was getting louder and Mike shouted to Jason. "Where are we going to next?"

"Target and then BestBuy."

"You do this every year?"

"Crazy isn't it?"

"Totally!"

As the elevator announced their arrival on the third floor of the office building that housed the doctor's office where Janet worked part-time. Jason and Rachel walked into the reception area of a modest sized office suite. From the listing on the glass window near the front door it looked like the office was a group practice of several chiropractors and several more massage therapists.

Janet Tabor's name was the third from the bottom. A small bell on the glass door rang and announced their arrival. A diminutive woman walked out from behind a screen and smiled. Her nametag read, 'Mary'. "Hello, are you here for an appointment?"

Jason smiled back. "Yes, we're here to see Janet Tabor. We have a two o'clock appointment with her."

"Oh yes, Jason Davies and Rachel Clark. Which one of you is going first?"

Rachel settled in a seat in the reception area and picked up a magazine. "Why don't you go first sweetie, I'll wait right here."

The receptionist turned and disappeared behind the screen again. A moment later Janet appeared. She looked radiant.

Rachel pulled her into a tight hug and whispered into her ear. "Was it as wonderful as you imagined?"

"Infinitely more," she whispered back.

Rachel released her and then Janet hugged Jason.

He paused a moment and looked into her eyes. "You look radiant, what happened after we left on Thursday?"

"I'll never tell," she whispered back and hugged him again. Then she stepped back and smiled. "So, who's going first?"

Jason raised his hand and grinned. "That would be me."

Janet ushered Jason around the screen towards the back of the office suite. "Come this way, sir. I'll be with you in an hour Rachel."

"No problem, I'll be here."

In the room Janet asked Jason to undress down to what he was comfortable with and get under the top sheet on the table. "I'll be back in just a moment."

"Okay, thanks."

Outside, Janet nearly raced down the hallway to collapse next to Rachel in a fit of giggles. She glanced around then whispered in her ear. "It was thee best sex I have ever had, ever!" Then she stood up quickly and dashed towards Jason leaving Rachel laughing at her jubilance. Janet almost skipped down the hallway.

A minute later Jason laid face down on the table with the sheet covering his legs. Janet composed herself and calmly came into the room. She adjusted the sheet around Jason and picked up her lotion. "So tell me if there is someplace I need to concentrate on."

"Just the usual spots, my upper and lower back are the most troublesome. I guess it's all from a bad case of 'computer hunch'."

"I get that all the time." Janet spread some lotion on his back and went to work kneading his sore muscles.

"So, here's a question for you." She paused a moment to work out a particularly tight muscle near his right shoulder blade. "Where did Jessie come from and why did you start cross-dressing?"

"Well, it's only cross-dressing technically."

"What do you mean?"

"From what I understand, most men who cross-dress, dress fully. I'm really only interested in the heels."

"Really, so no dresses or lingerie?"

"Nope."

"How did Rachel find out?"

Jason explained what happened the first day he moved into his apartment. How Rachel stepped over the dividing wall on their common terrace and sat down to paint his toenails red as a prank all the while thinking he was taking a nap.

"That's the craziest story I've ever heard. That girl's middle name has to be mischievous."

"I agree. Oh, yes, right there, that's where the knot is. Oof."

Janet moved around and began to work across his shoulders.

"The real moment came when she decided to put her four-inch high-heeled white sandals on my feet. She probably thought I would protest or fall over when I discovered what she'd done. But I didn't. She sat there dumbstruck as I casually stood up and walked to my terrace door. I turned with a grin and invited her in for a glass of iced tea."

"Unbelievable. I can imagine the look on her face."

"It was priceless. But she handled it all very well. In retrospect I can't believe that I even did that. I'm the epitome of the shy person when it comes to things like that."

"I'm glad you opened up. You guys have been so wonderful to Mike and me." She moved over to the other side and started working on his upper arm. "So where did Jessie come from?"

Jason explained about his twin sister Jessie, and why he decided on her name for when he was out shoe shopping with Rachel. "Jessie left us all way too early in life."

Janet's eyes began to glisten.

Jason shifted his leg to help Janet adjust the sheets as she dabbed her eyes.

"It's kind of nice knowing that my sister is still with me. I like to think that she's laughing at me all the while I'm standing there in high heels. She always was such a tease. She liked to point out that she was five minutes older than me, especially when she was trying to win an argument."

"So wearing heels was just a gift to Rachel? That's so incredibly sweet."

"That's why I never wanted to go anywhere but Sarah's shoe boutique. Jessie was supposed to be someone who was only with Rachel. But, things changed and that's okay too, as long as it goes no further.

"It won't, trust me."

"And, now Christmas is coming up and she wants me to go with her to her Christmas party where she works."

"As Jessie?"

"Yeah."

"How is she presenting you? Are you going to be her sister, or her cousin?"

"Crap. I think I've said too much already. Jan, you'll have to ask Rachel, she might kill me if I say anything else."

"Okay, let's bring her in." Janet walked to the door and peeked her head out. "Mary, can you ask Rachel Clark to come back to room nine? Thanks."

A moment later, Rachel knocked softly on the door and then opened it. She walked into the room and quietly shut the door. "Hi, you wanted to see me Jan?"

Before Janet could utter a word Jason interrupted her. "I'm sorry Rachel, it's just me and my big mouth. I was telling her about Jessie when it slipped out that Jessie was invited to attend a Christmas party at your work. She asked me how you're going to present me, as your sister or your cousin. That's when I said I couldn't say anymore without your permission."

"Did I step on a land mine here?"

Rachel smiled sweetly and sat down on a chair nearby. "No Jan, it's complicated. But you might as well know the whole story."

Rachel proceeded to explain the whole Rachel/Ray thing. How her work was so much easier if she dressed as Ray instead of Rachel. Then she told her about the night she was beat up and how Jessie took care of her.

"Somebody beat you up?"

"Yeah, he was a real Neanderthal." Rachel reached over and took Jason's hand. "It looked worse than it was and Jessie was just wonderful. So now my supervisor wants to meet Jessie, cause at work I'm Ray..."

Janet held up her hands and grinned. "Yeah, I got it. It is complicated isn't it?"

Rachel nodded. "And to make matters worse, Jason's Christmas party at his college is the same night and the Dean of Students wants to meet me as Rachel."

Janet stood with her mouth wide open. "How are you going to do that?"

Jason propped himself up on his elbows looking a bit bewildered. "I don't know but we'll manage somehow...changing in the backseat of a cab as we drive across town, maybe?"

"I can help."

They both responded simultaneously. "Huh?"

"I can help."

Rachel sat down on the bed next to Jason. "How?"

"When I was in college I worked as a dresser

backstage for the musical theatre department. I was a whiz at the quick change."

"Are you sure?"

"Of course! Come on, it'll be fun, I promise."

"But Mike can never know!"

Janet pulled Rachel and Jason into a big hug. "My lips are sealed."

TWENTY-SEVEN

It was the day before all the Christmas party craziness was supposed to happen and Rachel invited Janet over to her apartment under the pretense that she wanted help fitting the gown she bought for Jason's party, when actually, she was getting nervous and wanted a little moral support. There was a knock on the door and Rachel opened it. Janet crossed into her apartment and giving Rachel a little peck on the cheek as she passed by.

"We have a problem," Janet said as she flopped down on Rachel's couch.

Rachel opened the door to her refrigerator to retrieve a Coke. "What?"

"Mike just asked me to go to the faculty Christmas dinner with him."

Rachel lifted a bottle up to show Janet. "You want one?"

Janet shook her head. "No, thanks."

Rachel shut the refrigerator door. "Oh. That is a problem."

"Well, shit," Janet muttered and slumped her shoulders. "Now what?"

"Don't worry Jan, Jason and I will make do, we've managed before." Rachel sat down next to her on the couch.

"Yeah, I know…but I was sort of looking forward to it, like the old days in college. The scramble to change quickly, to not miss a beat and watch the actor waltz back out on stage in ten seconds or less."

Rachel sipped her coke. "Really?"

"Yeah, it was great. I think my most challenging change was in my senior year for *My Fair Lady*." Janet chuckled. "There was a quick change in the second act when Eliza Doolittle goes from an elegant gown, having just returned from the Embassy Ball, to a full set of traveling clothes in less than six measures."

"Six measures? How fast is that?"

"Fast," Janet said giggling. "Add to the fact that the girl playing the role looked like Audrey Hepburn. She had every stagehand in the theatre standing backstage ogling her, the poor thing. The idiots were hoping to catch a glimpse, but they didn't see a thing, I made sure of that!"

"How?"

"As she walked offstage, she stepped out of her heels and into a pair of character shoes, with a two-inch heel. They were placed in the center of her traveling outfit. As the ball gown went up over her head the traveling suit followed up from the floor. A quick button and a snap and she walked back on grabbing a suitcase along the way."

"Genius!"

"It was, but it took a week to practice in the

dressing room before we started technical rehearsals. She was a sweet little thing, and incredibly shy, so I did everything I could to help her out."

"Well, Jessie is just as shy but we won't be doing it in six measures. Our change is going to have to happen in the backseat of a rental van," Rachel said looking a bit concerned. "And we're going to have to swap drivers half way there so we can both change clothes."

"Damn," Janet muttered with a grimace. "I have to find a way to be a part of this. It'll be so much easier for you guys that way."

Rachel nudged Janet's shoulder. "You just want to see Jason in a dress, don't you?"

"Has he agreed to wearing one? The last I heard he flatly refused."

"He did, then I made a bet with him last Saturday and he lost," Rachel replied with a huge grin on her face. "He tried on a outfit we found at Macy's. The bodice is a black, cut lace poly-knit affair with a lace collar that's high on the neck. The ensemble has white lace on black velvet for the jacket and that goes over the bodice as well. The bottom is actually a wide set of pants in a tiny pleated poly-knit that looks like a gown when you're not walking, very full and incredibly sexy."

"He tried it on in the store?"

"Oh God no," Rachel said giggling. "His expression was murderous when I suggested that." She fell back against the sofa laughing. "We brought it home and he tried it on here."

"And?"

"Oh my God Jan, he looks stunning in it," she said grinning from ear to ear. "It was all I could do to

221

keep from tearing it off of him."

"Ooh, I want to see," Janet clapped her hands and laughed. "I have to find a way to help."

"My party starts at 7pm and Jason has to be at the college by 9:30 to hand out some awards. If we leave by 8:30 we'll have about thirty minutes to make the dash across town and change in the process to arrive in time to make the awards ceremony. Jason rented a commercial van last week to make it all happen. He wanted the panel style because it doesn't have any passenger windows."

"Hmm, good idea," Janet said, nodding. She paused a moment, lost in thought. "I think I've found a way around this." She turned to Rachel with a broad grin. "I'm going to call Mike and tell him that I have a last minute assignment at the design firm and that I'll just have to meet him at the banquet instead."

"He'll be disappointed," Rachel said leaning forward to touch her arm.

"I know, but I'll make it up to him later." Then her eyes began to sparkle. "Besides, I really want to see Jessie in that dress."

"Don't you dare tease him," Rachel replied.

"I won't, I promise." Janet grinned. "Hey, I want to see what you're going to wear."

"Ok, it's in the bedroom," Rachel replied taking Janet's hand and leading her down the hallway

Janet followed Rachel into her bedroom. Hanging from the closet door was a beautiful pearl white gown with white lace and tiny pearl embellishments.

Janet looked at the tag. "Adriana Papell, very nice, I simply love the seed pearls and lace." She pulled it off the closet door and walked over to

Rachel, holding it beneath her chin. "I can't wait to see you in this."

"Okay." Rachel blushed as she draped the gown across her bed then began to remove her clothes. She was down to her underwear before she realized that she was undressing in front of Janet for the first time. But before she could cover herself Janet saw the telltale sign of excitement building in her crotch.

"Oh my God, Rachel," Janet squealed and hugged her tightly. "I never knew you were just like me. You guys are like the brother and sister I never had!" She hugged her again, tightly. "I love you Rachel. You guys are my true family. Don't ever go away, okay?"

"We won't, I promise," Rachel replied hugging her back. "But," she paused blushing profusely, "I'm not quite what you think."

"What do you mean?"

Rachel sat down on her bed. She smiled meekly and stammered a bit. "I-I'm both."

Worry lines etched across Janet's brow as she moved the dress out of her way and sat down on the bed next to her. "I don't understand."

"I'm different, not a boy or a girl. They call it intersexed now. The old word was hermaphrodite. I'm both."

Janet took Rachel's hand, transfixed by what she said. "Both?"

"Yeah, I was born this way. I'm both…male and female," Rachel added meekly.

Janet sat looking into Rachel's eyes and a subtle smile grew into a broad grin as the full impact of what and whom she was became clear. "Rachel Clark, you are simply amazing." She drew Rachel into another big hug and squeezed her tight. "Oh my God, I'm so lucky to have you for a friend."

"But no one can know, not even Mike…promise?"

Janet crossed her heart. "I promise."

Jason walked into his apartment and dropped his briefcase by the front door. Rachel was already leaning against the terrace doorway with two glasses of wine. She knew from a cryptic message Jason texted to her earlier that it hadn't been a good day. Some of his students tried cheating on an essay exam and he caught them.

"I guess it's going to get ugly," he said taking a glass of wine Rachel offered. "Thanks." He turned and looked out across the barren trees and the apartment parking lot below. "Students don't realize what happens these days when they get caught cheating. They could get kicked out of school. To them, it's no big deal. But when they find themselves still living in mom's basement when they're thirty, they'll realize that it is. And of course, then they'll blame me for it."

Rachel leaned forward and planted a kiss on his cheek. "Welcome home, sweetheart, supper will be ready in a little bit."

She stepped back out the terrace door and walked toward her apartment.

"Dinner here or there, love?"

"My place, is that all right?"

He nodded and she ducked into her apartment as he slid his terrace door shut.

The dinner was light, mostly a garden salad and some homemade minestrone soup.

After dinner, Jason sat fussing about the cheating, his chin planted firmly in his hand propped up by his elbow. "The thing is, it was so obvious. Blatant quotes! Do they think teachers are stupid?"

Rachel stood up and cleared the dishes off the table then she walked barefoot back around the island counter and took Jason by the hand to lead him over to the couch.

He was still so caught up in the cheating incident that he failed to notice that she was slowly, provocatively, undoing the buttons on her blouse. Finally, still oblivious to her seduction, Rachel held his head in her hands and planted a kiss on his lips.

"I thought I'd wet your appetite for dessert, dear," she murmured as she trailed kisses up along his neck to his lips.

He raised his hands up to cup her cheeks and gently kissed her lips. "You are the most wonderful girl in the world. Nothing else matters when I'm in your arms."

"Hmm," she murmured and tenderly kissing his lips, "unless you're distracted."

"A momentary lapse, my love."

She kissed him on the nose, then his eyelids, then down his face to his ear. "Relax my sweet, and drift with me while I make love to you. Just let me caress you softly." She unbuttoned his shirt, sliding it off his shoulders and away. His chest, smooth and silky, quivered under her touch, his nipples stood proud as she grazed them with her nails.

"Tomorrow is going to be crazy, isn't it? I can't believe you made me lose that bet," he muttered with a grimace.

"I didn't make you lose that bet," she grinned as

she leaned in and kissed him on his cheek. "You did that all on your own. Besides, that gown looks stunning on you. All these months I believed your fibs when you told me you looked like a gorilla in drag. You are gorgeous sweetheart, I'm going to have to use a stick on all those horny lawyers at the party."

"Oh God," he groaned, "those two who hit on us in that Italian restaurant. They will be there, won't they?"

"Oh, I'm sure. And they're still just as clueless and single. But don't worry," she murmured, nuzzling up to his ear and whispering, "I'll be sure to keep my little girl safe."

"And I'll do the same at the college," he replied squirming under her caresses. "Some of my more lecherous colleagues will be drooling in their soup when they see you in that gown we bought. Oh, that tickles," he said grabbing her into hug.

"I think it's time for dessert," she murmured.

He started to speak again but she moved her finger to his lips with a gentle "shush." He moaned as she bent down and took another nipple into her mouth, gently nipping and sucking them into submission.

She stood up and pulled him off the sofa. They walked into her bedroom and she turned to kiss him.

Then she ran her hands across his chest and down to his slacks. She unbuckled them and let them crumple at his feet. She stood back up to unbutton her dress but Jason moved her hands away. "Let me," he said sweetly and he slowly undressed her. He slipped it over her shoulders and tossed it on the chair behind them then he reached behind her to unfasten her bra. His hands were trembling and

Rachel could feel his excitement. She leaned forward and kissed him gently on the lips then she hugged him. "My sweet, I know you always enjoy this as much as me." She leaned forward and whispered softly in his ear, "I love you."

"I love you too," he said as he knelt down in front of her. He placed his hands on her panties then lowered them down to fall at her feet. Her cock, now free from the confines of her lingerie, stood hard and proud against her stomach already rigid with anticipation. It pulsed with the throb of her heartbeat. He leaned forward and kissed her gently on the underside of her cock. She reached down and lifted him to his feet.

He pushed the covers off the bed and then he settled into the pillows on his back to watch her as she slipped on a condom from the drawer in the nightstand. She reached over and picked up a bottle of lube and slicked her condom-covered cock slowly, seductively, watching him watch her. She moved her lithe body onto the bed. Her long hair was flowing around her head and shoulders; it shimmered in the moonlight filtering through the blinds of her bedroom window.

She helped him move down the bed and she placed a pillow beneath his butt. She watched him open his legs to her.

"You are so beautiful, my love," she whispered. "The thought of being inside you fills me with such joy." She coated his rosebud with lube and slipped one and then another finger inside him. She watched him close his eyes and drift with the pleasure.

She positioned her cock at his entrance and rubbed against his anus for a moment then she pushed gently, entering him slowly. She could feel every ridge and muscle as she moved past his outer ring. Her cock pulsed and throbbed in tune with her heartbeat as his body stretched to accommodate her girth.

She looked into his eyes as she pushed gently forward. She pulled back out and added more lubricant then she pushed back into him again going deeper this time. She continued slowly until her body pressed against him. She rested a moment and kissed him tenderly on the lips.

"It feels marvelous," he murmured.

Several more thrusts and she filled her condom with her seed. She crushed her breasts against his chest as she wrapped her arms around him.

"My God, you make me feel complete," she whispered. She didn't want to soften. She wanted to stay inside of him forever but she knew it would happen eventually.

She sighed contentedly as she slowly slipped from his body. She pulled the condom off, tied the end, and let it fall into the wastebasket.

They lay quietly for a moment, listening to the other breathe softly in the stillness of the room. Finally, Rachel leaned up on one elbow. She leaned forward and kissed him, and then leaned back.

"I found a solution the other day for your profile. I ordered them online and they arrived today."

"What's that?"

"I bought some fake boobs for you, nothing huge, just enough to give a hint."

"I don't have to shave my chest do I?"

"Not unless you want to. Besides," she said

running her fingers across his chest, "I kind of like to play with your chest hair."

"Hmm, let's see them," he said sitting up in the bed.

"Okay." She leaned over and retrieved a small box with a classic portrait of a woman on it. She opened it and pulled out two silicone breast forms. "You can use one of my bras to hold them in place."

"Thanks. Make it an old one, I don't want to yank it all out of shape."

"You won't, we're almost the same size anyway," she said.

"Almost," he said cupping one of her beautiful breasts.

"With these you will be," she offered with a giggle. "Come on, let's try on the bra first then we'll slip the forms in place once you're fitted."

She got out of bed and rummaged around in the bottom of her lingerie drawer. "Here's one," she said pulling a black lace bra from the bottom of the drawer and looking at the label. "I was still a "B" cup when I bought this one so it should work on you nicely." She slipped his arms through the straps and reached around to fasten the clasp on his back.

He nuzzled her neck and ear while she adjusted the bra straps.

"You make it very hard to do this," she said giggling and squirming from his caresses.

"I can't help it, beautiful," he whispered. "You just filled me with your love and I feel so wonderfully fucked I'm not going to come back to earth for the rest of the night."

She opened the box and giggled as she stuffed the falsies into his bra cups. She leaned back and admired the way the bra fit him. She reached forward and cupped his fake breasts; they jiggled as she moved them.

"Oh my, seeing you with tits is having an interesting effect on me," she said looking down at her growing cock.

"Hmm," Jason said leaning back against some pillows, his new tits pushed up prominently, "I'm ready again if you are, darling." She slipped on another condom as he lifted his leg and straddled her. She lifted her hips slightly and entered him again in one thrust.

=TWENTY-EIGHT=

Rachel leaned out of the bathroom and looked at Jessie pulling on her pant-skirt. "What shoes are you wearing?"

"Those black Rachel Roy's, is that okay?"

"Perfect, then I'm going to borrow the Sergio Rossi's for the college party," she said ducking back into the bathroom and applying another dab of concealer under her eyes. "If I don't find a workable fix with those servers soon I am going to lose even more sleep. I have bags on my bags."

Jessie leaned in and kissed her on the cheek. "Oh, you do not. But don't go too heavy with that concealer or Ray will have some explaining to do."

Jessie slipped on the bra Rachel loaned her and stuffed the falsies into each cup. "I'm ready for you to do your magic, sweetheart."

"God, you look sexy in a bra," she grinned. "Why don't you start with the foundation and I'll help you finish up after I get my suit on."

Jessie blushed and gave her an air-kiss then

turned and sat at the dressing table. Several minutes later she'd managed to complete her foundation and eyebrows. Then she started on her eyes.

Ray stepped over and knelt down next to her. "You're really getting good at this. A little blush and you're almost done." She picked up a bottle of eyeliner. "Let me help."

Once Ray finished the eyeliner he stepped back as Jessie stood up. She pulled on her jacket and turned slowly. "Here, I have just the thing to complete this." He dashed to the jewelry box across the room and pulled out a ruby colored necklace with a gold colored chain. "It's costume jewelry but it looks almost as good as the real thing."

"Will anyone be able to tell?"

"The lawyers won't." Ray shrugged his shoulders a bit and smirked. "Maybe their wives will but who cares, nobody will be looking up here anyway, babe, you look hot!" He patted her on the ass.

Jessie leaned forward and kissed Ray on the lips. "You are biased, my love. I still look like a gorilla in drag."

"Shush. Now grab those garment bags, we have to go." Ray pulled on his coat and grabbed a clutch purse from the dresser. "We can share. You can use it at the law office and I'll use it at the college party."

"Perfect. Wait, what do you have in there?"

Ray grinned. "Makeup, your car keys, some tissues, and a tampon."

"A tampon?"

"Of course! What girl would leave the house without planning for emergencies? Now come on, we're going to be late."

Jessie carried two dress bags with her to the car then she got into the passenger side as Ray held the door for her. Ray leaned over and murmured. "Every guy in that office is going to be jealous when they see what a hot date I have on my arm."

Jessie blushed as Ray walked around the car and slipped in behind the wheel.

The company party was already in full swing when Ray and Jessie arrived on the third floor. Before the elevator doors opened they could hear the thump of music coming from the commons room beyond reception.

Ray leaned over and kissed a worried Jessie on the cheek. "Don't worry, sweetie, you look stunning." The elevator doors opened and they stepped into the corridor. Ahead several people were gathered near the reception desk. One of them was Ray's supervisor, Oscar.

As they approached the office door Oscar turned with a broad smile. "Ray, Feliz Navidad amigo, it's great to see you." He shook Ray's hand and turned to see Jessie standing nearby. The smile on his face beamed brightly. "And who's this? The mysterious girlfriend, Jessie?" He reached forward with both hands to shake Jessie's.

"Oscar," Ray said, her voice somewhat lower than normal. "This is Jessie, my neighbor and a very special friend."

"It's nice to meet you," Jessie said as softly as she could.

"And you too," Oscar said taking both their hands. "Ray's told me so much about you, but he didn't say what a gorgeous woman you were," Oscar added a slap on Ray's shoulder for emphasis. "Come on, amigos, the party's already started. The drinks are over there and there's snacks on the table over there," he said pointing to the locations as they walked into the room. "Everyone, Ray is here with his friend Jessie." Oscar placed a little bit of emphasis on the word 'friend' when speaking about Jessie.

Jessie blushed a bit after Oscar's introduction. The last thing she wanted to do was jeopardize Ray's job by embarrassing her. She smiled a bit and nodded to others as they shouted 'hello'. Then she leaned over to Ray and whispered. "I think I'm going to need a stiff drink."

Ray smiled and replied. "Relax girl, you look fantastic."

Jessie glanced around the room. Everyone seemed to be having a great time and no one appeared to notice anything out of the ordinary. "Easy for you to say, you're incredible. I, on the other hand, will probably trip on my way to get that drink."

"Don't be silly, you've walked in those shoes a hundred times. Come on, let me introduce you." Ray steered her towards a refreshments table and several older gentlemen in suits. "Bob, Harvey, I'd like you to meet Jessie, a very close friend of mine. Jessie, this is Bob Reynolds, he's one of the senior partners, and this is Harvey Wallace, he handles some of the corporate accounts."

Jessie extended her hand and smiled shyly.

Bob gave her a hearty handshake. "You're the girl who helped Ray when he had that accident, right?"

Jessie smiled meekly and nodded.

Harvey gestured to the drinks table. "Would you folks like something to drink?"

Jessie nodded and tried to speak softly. "Bourbon, neat, single vat if you have it."

Ray glanced at Jessie. He pursed his lips into a tiny smirk.

Harvey grinned. "Really?" He held up a bottle for Jessie's inspection. "Will this do?"

Jessie smiled. "Yes, that's very nice, thank you."

Ray squeezed Jessie's hand. "I'll have a glass of white wine please. Thank you."

More guests arrived and the two gentlemen stepped over to greet them leaving Ray and Jessie alone for a moment.

Jessie looked into Ray's eyes and whispered. "I'm so nervous." She glanced around the room, "Do you think I did something wrong?"

"You mean about the bourbon?"

Jessie nodded.

"No. I think Harvey was impressed. I know I was."

A piano began to play a jazzy Christmas tune in the background. Ray set his drink down and took Jessie's hand. "Come on sweetheart, let's dance."

They moved out into an area cleared of desks and chairs, joining several other couples. Ray leaned forward and whispered into Jessie's ear. "You rather good at letting me lead."

"It's only fair," she whispered back. "I'll get to lead at the college later."

A moment later someone tapped Ray on the shoulder. "Do you mind if I cut in?"

Ray nodded and gave up Jessie's hand.

Jessie's eyes grew large as she realized that it was

one of the lawyers who hit on them at the Italian restaurant a while back. She glanced over to Ray who stood and shrugged.

"Hi, I'm Rob, have we met before?" His hand slipped below her waist to rest on her left butt cheek.

"I don't think so," Jessie replied, reaching back to raise his hand back to her waist.

"Wait a minute. I remember now," Rob said, moving his hand back down to her butt. "You were at an Italian restaurant with some other girl."

"Oh, yes, I guess I was." Jessie pulled Rob's hand back up and shook her head.

"But I thought you were a lesbian?"

Jessie smiled demurely and shrugged her shoulders. "If I remember correctly, the girl I was out with that night was my sister. I said I was in a committed relationship, you must have assumed it was with her."

"Oh, okay. That's probably it." he said, looking somewhat bewildered.

The music ended and Jessie shook Rob's hand. "Thank you." She turned and spotted Ray near the refreshments table.

As she moved toward Ray another familiar face intercepted her, wrapping his arm around her waist.

"Hi, I'm Bill. Can I have your picture so I can show Santa what I want for Christmas?" His hand slipped from her waist to cup her butt. He winked at her and leaned in to kiss her cheek.

Jessie slipped out of his grasp as Bill leaned too far forward and he ended up kissing the door behind her with a loud thump. Jessie shook her head and walked briskly over to Ray. "Lawyers are handsy," she snorted under her breath.

"Yes they are," Ray replied through his smile. "Now you know why I'm Ray."

Oscar, his supervisor approached. "Ray, buddy, you should try the snacks. They even have caviar."

"Please excuse me," Jessie said, "I need to use the restroom."

Oscar pointed off to the left. "We have only one but don't be alarmed, it only has stalls."

"Thanks." Jessie moved off through the throng of people nodding and smiling as others said 'Merry Christmas'.

She closed one of the stalls in the unisex restroom then she slipped her pant-skirt off to sit down on the stool.

A moment later she heard two men enter the restroom. She overheard them step up to the sinks at the end of the room. One of them remarked: "Damn. That's one hot piece of ass. How'd Ray tap that?"

Jessie pulled off a piece of tissue to dab herself then she pulled up her pant-skirt and adjusted her blouse.

"I had no idea IT guys had that much going for them. He must have some serious junk. You know what I mean?"

Jessie stepped between the two men at the sink. They have no idea, she thought, a smirk slipping across her lips. No idea at all.

Both men looked at one another then they quickly turned and reached for towels.

Jessie leaned into the mirror and ran her little finger across her eyebrow. Then she turned and walked out of the restroom with a smirk planted firmly on her lips. The click of her heels on the

237

marble floor the only sound that could be heard.

As Jessie stepped out of the restroom she spotted Ray across the room, at the refreshments table, talking to Oscar. She walked towards the table to join them. But before she could reach them, Rob, her inept dance partner, stepped up and slapped Oscar on the shoulder.

"Have you seen Ray's date," Rob asked, his speech a bit slurred from too much alcohol. "She's hot."

Before he could prevent it, Oscar's drink flew from his hand and landed square into Ray's chest. His shirt was drenched and soaking through quickly.

Jessie moved quickly across the room and whipped her jacket off to cover Ray's chest, hopefully before anything could be revealed.

"Let's get you to the restroom before the stain sets in," Jessie said.

Rob stood dumbfounded, weaving a bit unsteady against the drinks table. "What happened? Did I do that?"

"I am so sorry," Oscar said. "It just slipped."

"I know, Oscar, it's okay." Ray said as Jessie quickly led him away and towards the restroom.

They stepped inside the restroom and ducked into a stall.

Jessie pulled off her coat and Ray opened up his suit jacket. "Does it show?"

"Not yet, but let's not take any chances," Jessie said. "Is there a back way out of here?"

"Yes, right around the corner there's a fire escape that leads to the parking garage a couple of floors down. Our coats are on a chair near the exit."

"Perfect. Can you text Janet and tell her we're

on our way?"

Ray nodded and pulled out his cellphone. Then, just before stepping out of the restroom stall, Ray reached into his pocket and pressed a fake moustache into place.

Jessie looked at him with a shocked expression. "What's that for?"

"Insurance. Security cameras are everywhere but not in a restroom. Come on love," he said grabbing her hand, "Janet's waiting."

Jessie opened a door for Ray as they retreated down the back stairway towards the garage several floors below. "Do you think they saw anything?"

Ray shook his head as he pulled Jessie's jacket off and handed it back to her. "Probably not. You whipped your jacket off so fast I doubt they even saw the punch land on my shirt," he said with a chuckle. "Besides I covered the rest up with my jacket." He pulled on his overcoat as they finished the last flight of stairs to the parking garage. He pointed overhead at the camera aimed at the stairway and winked at Jessie.

As they opened the exit door Janet pulled into a handicap spot near the entrance. She opened the sliding door on the side of the van wearing blue jeans, a sweatshirt, a ball cap, and a huge grin. "Hi girls! How was party number one?"

"Lawyer's are handsy," Jessie muttered as Rachel slipped behind the wheel with a grin and started the van. Jessie stepped into the back and Janet swung the side door shut.

Janet shook her head in amazement. "My God, Jessie, you look incredible in that dress!" I would never have recognized you."

Rachel gunned the motor and shouted. "Doesn't she? Don't believe a word she says about gorillas in drag!"

"Absolutely, the next time we get together I want to see you in this again! You look absolutely fabulous!"

Jessie blushed then shook her head a moment and turned to Janet. "Well, let's just hope that nobody else can recognize me," he said removing his jacket. "I think I saw Mike's white Honda peeking around the far corner on this level. He may have seen me get into this van."

"I think you're right but he won't know it's you." Janet leaned forward and touched Rachel's shoulder as she turned toward the exit. "Rachel, sweetheart, you're going to have to loose him on the way over."

"No problem, but hold on tight."

Janet turned back to help Jessie undo her bodice and two falsies popped out from behind her bra.

"Oops, sorry about that," Jessie muttered blushing crimson.

"No problem, before I got my permanent ones I had to use them all the time," she chuckled. "Never had them explode off my chest quite like that though."

The van slid through a corner before the final exit ramp and Janet slammed against Jessie trying to pull off his pant-skirt. They were being tossed around like loose boxes in a delivery van.

"Let's wait until Rachel can lose the Honda," Janet suggested and Jessie nodded.

"Sorry guys," Rachel shouted from the driver's seat. "I think you were right about that white Honda, it's right on my tail."

"Is it Mike?" Janet shouted above the squeal of tires protesting loudly. "Can he see you in the mirror?"

"I'm not sure, but with the fake moustache it probably doesn't matter," Rachel shouted back.

She turned another corner quickly and then darted into an alleyway. "Hold on guys, it's gonna be a bumpy ride until I lose him."

Trashcans bounced off the bumper and flew across the alley as rats scrambled into dumpsters.

The van slid across a sidewalk to skid into the street. It spun to the right and disappeared between two large trucks, weaving like an Indy car driver.

They raced down the street, turned left, and ducked into another alley. When the van exited onto the next street Rachel spun the wheel violently and the van spun to the left this time. It roared off on two wheels until it slammed back to the pavement.

"Holy Crap," Jason shouted. "You drive like you've done this before!"

Rachel grinned as she slowed for a red light and glanced into the rearview mirror. "Small town on a Saturday night, love. The local "Barney Fife" had a penchant for busting underage teens with a six-pack."

Jessie and Janet shook their heads. "I'm simply amazed at the thought of a teenage Rachel racing through streets and alleyways, out-running the local cops, her hair flying behind her like a rebel," Jessie shouted as Rachel grinned and gunned the van through another intersection.

At the next light, she turned to speed up an onramp to the freeway. She kept checking her mirrors but there was no immediate sign of Mike and his Honda. She slowed down a bit but decided to take the next exit anyway. It was easier to dodge and weave through a neighborhood than try to out-run a car on the freeway.

With the van moving at a steady pace, Jessie managed to get the rest of her pant-skirt and blouse off. Janet helped with his bra and then she pulled a t-shirt out to slip over his head.

Jessie, now quickly transforming to Jason, grabbed a dress shirt off a hanger but Janet held his wrist.

"Wait till we get the makeup off first sweetie," she said applying a tissue with makeup remover to his eyes. "You don't want it to rub off on that nice white shirt."

He nodded while she continued to wipe his mascara.

Jason grinned as she took another swipe off his face. "You're loving this, aren't you?"

"Oh my God, this is the best! I always seem to have so much fun when you two are around," she shouted over the roar of the motor. "Here's your shirt," she said. "Next we'll get your pants. You can do your shoes when she stops the van."

Jason slipped the shirt over his head and inadvertently revealed the lacy black panties he wore as Jessie.

"Sexy," she growled looking down with a broad grin.

"They matched the bra," Jason replied, his face glowing crimson. He pulled on one pant leg and then another.

At that moment Rachel pulled up to a spot behind Janet's car. She was parked on a side street several blocks away from the college.

"We're here." She jumped back to help put the finishing touches on Jason's transformation to a suit.

"I got all the makeup off I could see, Rach, but I need help with his fingernails," Janet said dabbing his eyes with makeup remover.

"No problem," Rachel said pulling her fake moustache off. "We used fake nails for that very reason."

"I can finish those up, Rachel," Jason said. "You need to get dressed. We're almost running late."

Rachel nodded as they changed places. She quickly removed her damp shirt and tie followed by her pants.

"Ho-ho! You two have matching underwear, how cute," Janet quipped.

Rachel smirked and shrugged. "Jan, help me with this zipper."

In a matter of minutes Janet managed to transform them both. Rachel finished her makeup and Jason helped her slip on her heels.

While Rachel and Jason finished up, Janet started her change from her work jeans to a gorgeous black satin strapless that clung to her curves like a kid glove.

Rachel leaned forward and gave Janet a peck on the cheek. "Jan, give us a couple of minutes so it doesn't look like we came together, okay?"

"No problem, Sis," Janet replied with a grin. "I still have to do my makeup."

They stepped out of the van, slid the door shut, and started the walk towards the Memorial Hall entrance where the celebration was going to take place.

"Sis?" Jason had a quizzical expression.

"She found out about me," Rachel replied

moving quickly in her heels. "But she's cool with it and promises to keep it a secret. We're sisters now, it was sweet."

"Okay. I guess it is hard to keep secrets from your friends, especially close ones. I guess that makes me worry a little about Mike."

They turned a corner and Memorial Hall was only a block away. "Probably," Rachel replied, "but if he's a true friend it won't matter."

Ahead, Mike was standing impatiently outside of the main entrance, glancing several times at this wristwatch.

He looked anxiously at Jason and Rachel as they walked up to the front door. "Hey guys, have you seen Janet?"

About then Janet turned the corner a block away and, walking briskly in her heels, she was at the front of the building in minutes and standing next to Mike a moment later. "Sorry Mike, I got here as fast as I could."

"That doesn't matter, babe, you look gorgeous," he glanced to Rachel and grinned. "You both do."

Janet leaned forward and kissed him as Rachel offered him a tiny curtsey. "Thanks, Mike."

Mike looked back to Jason. "Where's your car?"

"Huh? Oh, I left it at the apartment. We decided to take a cab, what with too much wine and all, you know on a night like this the cops will be out in droves."

"That's true. Come on, we're almost late."

Once inside, several members of the Dean's staff greeted them. "Professor Davies, the Dean wants you to come this way. The award ceremony is about to begin. You can rejoin your party after it's over." The staffer led Jason away from Rachel, Mike and Janet who moved off in the direction of the banquet area. Jason glanced back to see several of his colleagues and their wives greet Rachel, Mike and Janet. From the looks on the men's faces, Rachel and Janet were going to be the center of too much unwanted attention this evening.

At the podium, Jason announced a dozen student award winners, several for undergraduate research in various fields and others for academic excellence. Several faculty and staff awards followed this. They including meritorious service awards, recognition for nationally ranked peer-reviewed journals, and a few announcements for upcoming published books.

From Jason's point of view it felt like the award ceremony was going to last for hours but within minutes of the last staff recognition award the whole event was over.

Throughout the event, he kept a watchful eye on Rachel. Several of his meeker colleagues merely waved and offered a simple smile and a shrug, the rowdy bunch from the Criminal Justice Department on the other hand, were more brazen, even soliciting frowns from the Dean.

As Jason walked from the podium to his table he passed by the Criminal Justice table. He leaned down, clamped his hand on his colleague Professor Arnold's shoulder. He leaned in to whisper. "If you can't behave I will speak to classroom scheduling and you'll be holding your classes in the dungeon starting next week."

Arnold turned bright red then spun around in his chair and sputtered. "You can't do that!"

Jason leaned back down again and smiled maliciously. "Try me." Then he turned and smiled at Rachel as he meandered through several more tables towards his seat next to Rachel.

As Jason returned to the their table he leaned over and muttered to Mike. "It's one thing to admire a beautiful woman but God, academics have no shame when it comes to ogling!"

Mike shook his head. "You'd think that in a public institution filled with rules and regulations about sexual misconduct and harassment the clowns would at least behave in a public forum. What did you say to Arnold?"

"I suggested his classes might get moved to the dungeon. Monica owes me big time."

Mike grinned. "Doesn't she handle the weekly building schedules and classroom assignments?"

Jason nodded.

"That's evil."

"I know. He got all huffy but he also got the point." Jason turned to Rachel and leaned over to give her a peck on the cheek.

Rachel smiled and turned to Jason. "Apparently, academics are as bad as lawyers," she whispered.

"I did warn you," he grimaced with a shrug.

About then dessert was served.

Janet looked up and shrugged her shoulders. "I guess we missed dinner."

Mike nodded. "From what my colleagues said, it wasn't worth the effort. Rubber chicken breasts and breadsticks as hard as railroad spikes."

Before Jason could act to prevent it, Randy Billingsley from the Earth Science Department, also one of the award recipients, pulled up a chair. He squeezed in between Jason and Rachel. "Hi beautiful, I'm Randy Billingsley." Jason tapped him on the shoulder and Randy turned around in his seat. "Hey, it's the prerogative of the guy who gets an award," he said smugly then he turned back to Rachel. "So, what can a Scientist do that an English professor can't?" Randy winked at Rachel and glanced back at Jason who was on a slow boil. "Play by all the numbers," he snickered walking his fingers up her arm.

Before Jason could stand, Rachel leaned over and spoke softly to Randy. "Academics are just as bad as lawyers. Speaking of lawyers, I have a friend who specializes in workplace relations." She offered him a menacing smile. "Should I give her a call?"

Randy's face went ashen as he shook his head and quickly moved away from the table.

Mike leaned over and spoke softly to Rachel. "I'm sorry Rachel, not all my colleagues behave this badly, I guess alcohol brings out the worst in them."

"That's all right Mike, no matter where you work, the demographics are the same. Certain percentages are assholes and certain percentages are saints. Gladly, for Janet and me, we are lucky enough to know the latter."

"Thanks," Mike replied.

The rest of the evening was uneventful. The Dean offered his holiday wishes to the college. A toast followed that, and the rest of the party dissolved into small pockets of conversation.

Shortly afterwards, the Dean and his wife walked over to Jason's table. Jason introduced Rachel and Mike introduced Janet.

"So happy to see you here, my dear," the Dean offered cordially while shaking Rachel's hand. He turned to Janet and shook her hand as well. "Merry Christmas."

The Dean turned back to Rachel. "I understand you work in Information Technology, do you have an advanced degree?"

Rachel smiled and nodded. "I'm a system administrator with a law office downtown and I have a masters degree in computer science with an emphasis in systems engineering from The University of Maryland."

The Dean blinked a bit surprised. "Have you considered teaching?"

Rachel smiled. "I haven't – should I?"

"Perhaps you should," the Dean replied. "I'll speak to Henry, the Dean of Computer Sciences, about it next week and see if he has any openings. It may be part-time at first but you never know." He turned to Mike and Jason. "Merry Christmas to you all and," he said looking at Jason and Mike, "I'll see you both in January."

As the Dean and his wife walked away Rachel glanced at Jason and blushed. "I guess I told a little fib when I said I hadn't been away from home except for a trip to DC with my parents."

Jason nodded. "I remember you did mention that when we first met."

"Well, the master's program was mostly online and I had to do two summer semesters in residence on the main campus in College Park. It was almost like I wasn't there so I guess I never counted it as being away from home. Sorry."

"No worries," Jason said hugging her shoulders. "A master's in computer science is impressive. You're sort of overqualified to be working at the law office aren't you?"

Rachel nodded. "It was what I could find locally and still, sort of, stay in my line of work."

"If the offer presents itself, do you want to teach?"

"I'd consider it," she replied. "I'd have to do a little brushing up – things change quickly in this field. At least our vacation time would coincide."

Jason leaned over and kissed her on the cheek.

Mike tapped Jason on the shoulder. "Let's get out of here, this place is getting stuffy. Remind me again why we don't hang out with our colleagues?"

Jason nodded and they all moved quietly towards the exit.

Outside, they walked towards a fountain at the head of a commons area adjacent to several classroom buildings. It was now bone dry with winter firmly at hand. They sat on some benches that surrounded the fountain and gazed up into the clear night sky.

"This has been one crazy evening," Rachel said, laughing.

Jason turned to his friend as he leaned back and looked into the night sky. "Mike, how come you were outside before we got here? Did you have something else to do that kept you from arriving before the banquet started?"

Rachel elbowed Jason in the ribs and he smirked.

Mike sighed. "Well, I was supposed to escort Janet, but she had a last minute job at the design firm."

"Sorry, Mike," Janet added.

"It's okay. Actually, I decided to drop by her design office earlier this evening to help out if I could.

Then I saw a van whip by me heading for a parking garage and I thought I saw Janet driving. So I decided to follow."

"Really," Janet said. "Someone who looked like me?" She glanced sideways at Rachel and Jason.

"Well, no, not exactly. I only got a glimpse and the driver was wearing a ball cap so it was hard to tell, they went by so quickly. But it kind of looked like you."

Jason glanced at Janet and Rachel with a grin.

"I decided to follow and get a better look," Mike continued. "When I got to the second floor of the parking deck the van had pulled up to a loading zone and I think several people got in. I couldn't see who it was because the van blocked my view."

Janet leaned forward. "So did you just leave after that?"

Mike shook his head. "No. Once the people got in, the van raced off suspiciously so I decided to follow. I was getting curious."

Jason turned and leaned around Janet to look at Mike. "Did you catch up with the van?"

"Hell no, they drove like crazy," Mike exclaimed. "Through alleyways, and across traffic. They might have even run a few lights. I lost them after I came out of the second alley." Mike shook his head and chuckled. "That driver was one crazy lunatic."

Janet, Jason, and Rachel smiled and nodded.

They were silent for a moment, listening to the sounds of a winter's night.

Then Jason stood up, turned, and knelt down in front of Rachel. He took Rachel's hand in his and produced a small velvet covered box from his coat pocket. Rachel's breath caught. She was beaming with tears cascading down her cheeks all in the same moment. Janet's eyes were glistening and Mike was grinning.

"Rachel, my love, I can't begin to express how much my life has changed since that moment on the terrace so many months ago. I know something like this may seem rash to some but I am beyond certain that I want to spend the rest of my life with you, if you'll have me."

He opened the ring box. Inside a single solitaire diamond mounted on a gold band stood prominently displayed. "Would you marry me?"

"Yes, yes, yes!" She wrapped her arms around his neck and squeezed then kissed him passionately. "Yes!"

Jason turned to Mike and Janet with a huge smile. "I guess we're getting married."

Mike clapped Jason on the back and laughed. Then he paused with a curious look in his eye. "Is that eyeliner in your eyes?"

Janet hands shot to cover the smirk on her lips as Rachel snickered.

TWENTY-NINE

Epilogue...

One week later, after a lovely lunch at Hanna and Bob's place, Rachel and Jason returned to host Mike and Janet for a charming Christmas dinner at his apartment. The dinner had all the fixings one would expect on the table of a traditional Christmas feast.

After the dessert was served, Mike reached across the table and took Janet's hands in his. "Janet, my life was never been filled with more joy than it was the day you agreed to go out with me. But each night we're together I hate having to leave you to come home to an empty house."

Janet nodded, her eyes glistening. "Me too."

"Would you like to move in with me?"

"Yes," she whispered as she curled into his arms. "Besides, your stove works and mine doesn't," she added with a grin.

Mike laughed and hugged her tightly. "Is that the only reason?"

Janet grinned. "I can think of a few more." She nuzzled his neck and kissed him on the cheek.

Resting her head on Mike's shoulder, she looked over at Jason and Rachel. "I love you guys, you two are the best friends a girl could ever have."

"I couldn't agree more," Mike added, "Merry Christmas."

Jason and Rachel's wedding was in May, right after Jason's finals. It was simple affair but very elegant.

Karen and her family flew in from Cleveland, Rachel's sister and her husband Bob and the kids were there too. Her Mom and Dad even made the trip up from Florida.

Janet was Rachel's maid of honor and Mike stood up with Jason. They flew to Paris and honeymooned on a cruise ship down the Rhone River.

Janet moved in with Mike right after Christmas and Jason and Rachel are looking for a house to buy together. One of the must haves is a terrace with a view.

Oh, and they started some preliminary paperwork with a local adoption agency. Jason would be happy with two but Rachel is hoping for more. All in all, sleeping on the terrace turned out to be the start of something truly wonderful.

ABOUT THE AUTHOR:

GUY WINTERS is a writer, playwright, and artist, who spends his days working in Virginia, and his evenings writing.

If you're into paranormal romance, checkout these newly release novels,

Vampire Rain

After his wife died, Alex thought his life was permanently on hold until he met a girl considering suicide as she sat in the rain. Emma forever changed his life. She was the beautiful Vampire Halfling he met that night. From the mundane world of academia, he's thrust into a violent struggle for survival in a battle between vampire and dhampir. PG-13 for language and violence.

Vampire Rain is a story about vampires, and it's a story about trust.

But most of all, It's a story about love.

or

Vampire + Love

Ian McIntyre thought his vampire romance book was just a lark, a romantic adventure with a twist. He knew that vampires were a myth. He brushed off would be admirers with a scoff, "Vampires are just a figment of our imagination." And that's what he thought, until he met one.

Dangerous and beautiful, Naomi is an intoxicating combination that even he couldn't resist, and she needs his help.

Other erotic novels by GUY WINTERS include:

Once Upon A Bite So Sweet,

Enjoy this adult romp of a vampire tale with a quirky twist. Forget the myths, they're all wrong. The vampires are more human; the sexual tension between Alicia and Jacob is electric; and Jacob's worldview has just taken a quantum leap. Vampires with a moral imperative! Go figure! An adult novella with explicit sex and language. Not intended for readers under 18 years of age.

Stray Cats

"We three are like Stray Cats wandering through our lives looking for love and tenderness. We are who we are because of our past and love has brought us together for our future. Alex kissed them both. "Thank you." Enjoy this Adult Erotic Novella redefining family. It is intended for Mature Readers only."

Dark Places

A romantic story of a college professor who doesn't quite know how lonely his life has become, searching for a transgendered women to interview for his thesis project. Suddenly running into someone who makes him understand just what kind of a job he's bitten off. She propels him into far darker places than he was really ready to be taken.

They are available at Smashwords.com and other fine eBook distributors.